*By Janie Bolitho*

Snapped in Cornwall
Framed in Cornwall
Buried in Cornwall
Betrayed in Cornwall
Plotted in Cornwall
Killed in Cornwall
Caught Out in Cornwall

# BURIED IN CORNWALL

## JANIE BOLITHO

Allison & Busby Limited
12 Fitzroy Mews
London W1T 6DW
*allisonandbusby.com*

First published in Great Britain in 1999.
This paperback edition published by Allison & Busby in 2015.

A CIP catalogue record for this book is available from
the British Library.

10 9 8 7 6 5 4 3 2

ISBN 978-0-7490-1964-8

Typeset in 10.5/15.5 pt Sabon by
Allison & Busby Ltd.

The paper used for this Allison & Busby publication
has been produced from trees that have been legally sourced
from well-managed and credibly certified forests.

Printed and bound by
CPI Group (UK) Ltd, Croydon, CR0 4YY

*For my grandson,*
*Matthew James Bolitho*

# CHAPTER ONE

'You've made a real fool of yourself this time.'

Rose Trevelyan closed her eyes and took a deep breath. No need to ask who was calling, she knew that voice well enough. Anger and humiliation fought for supremacy.

'Especially now. God, you must've read enough articles in the *Western Morning News* about time-wasters. You know, people who ring triple nine when they break a nail or can't find their glasses. People like you, Rose.'

'End of lecture?' she asked sweetly, trying to show how little she cared for his opinion of her.

'Why on earth did you do it? Do you know how much that whole exercise cost?'

No, she thought, but you're about to tell me. He did, and it was an awful lot of money. How many emotions could she cope with at once? Guilt had now joined in the struggle with humiliation and anger. Never explain, never apologise, someone had once said. Rose had no intention of doing the latter but she still felt an unreasonable need to do the former, to justify herself to the man who had once promised her so much and whom she had wrongly blamed for not living up to her expectations. It was she who had not been ready to make a commitment. Rose knew what he was thinking, that in this, as in their personal life, she would refuse to take the blame. 'I heard something, I really did.'

'Too much red wine, I expect.' And with that the line went dead.

Anger won. It was more than anger, it was rage. Red-faced, she paced the room, chewing at a fingernail. 'Sod you, Jack Pearce,' she said aloud, feeling the prickling of tears behind her eyelids.

With a shake of her head, she went to the kitchen and, to spite Jack, opened a bottle of Medoc. She took the glass into the sitting room and sipped the wine as she surveyed what had become her world from the window. Warmth from the fire she had lit in the grate complemented that of the small radiator beneath the curved window which overlooked Mount's Bay. Darkness was already descending, coming earlier each day as Christmas drew nearer. St Michael's Mount in the distance was no more than a sinister jagged rock outlined blackly against the striated colours of the sky. The horizon was tinged a whitish yellow as the sun sank further into the west. The clouds were purple, a shade deeper than that of the heather which bloomed on the cliffs that ran down to the sea. The last fingers of light edged them in brilliant orange.

A few cars, unseen below Rose's steeply sloping garden, passed from Mousehole down into Newlyn, but she could see the tops of those coming up the hill. One slowed, and the arc of its headlights briefly illuminated the front of the house as it pulled into the drive. She swore aloud in the language of the fishermen with whom she often drank. The view which, day or night, winter or summer, was always able to restore her equanimity had done its work. The appearance of Jack Pearce, Inspector Jack Pearce, had destroyed it again. She heard a rapping on the kitchen door. It was at the side of the house and opened on to the garden. She could, of course, refuse to answer it even though the door was unlocked and the kitchen light was on. Jack knew that she was in and that the door was rarely locked but he also knew better than to walk in uninvited. It would be cowardly to ignore him. Her affair with Jack was over, although he found it hard to accept, but that was no reason to behave in anything other than an adult manner. She had nothing to fear from him. Besides, in a way she owed him something. It was Jack who had shown her that she was able to feel again. Five years after David had died he had come into her life and proved that there could be someone else. The months of David's lingering death were not a period of her life she would ever forget but she had learnt to accept the finality and had put it behind her as belonging only to her memory. Initially she had thought that to get involved with another man would be to diminish what she and David had shared, which was over twenty years of happiness. Later she had learnt that no one or nothing could take that away from either of them. In retrospect it seemed calculating to admit that Jack had served his purpose. Metaphorically he had brought her back to life and made her strong enough to live it alone. Jack had wanted permanency, Rose only wanted to feel alive again. There was no question that she had enjoyed his company: the laughter and the arguments, the spark which had existed between them and the nights they had spent together. But that, too, was in the past.

She let him knock a second time before crossing the narrow flagstoned hallway and going to open the kitchen door. Through the glass she saw Jack's large, familiar figure as he stood rubbing his hands together. She let him in. With him came cold air so she quickly shut the door. That indefinable feeling, that *frisson* which had existed between them, had not completely disappeared, Rose realised as his bulk filled the room and she looked up, allowing herself a brief glimpse of his dark, handsome Cornish face.

Warmth flooded her neck and cheeks when his own eyes dropped pointedly to the glass she still held in her hand. It was so unfair. Most evenings when she had finished work she opened some wine. Why did Jack always have to catch her in the act and make it seem like a sin? 'Why are you here?'

'I wanted to make sure you were all right.' In a manner which suggested he was more than at home in her kitchen he folded his arms and leant back against the cooker. Rose wished it was on. Full on.

She snorted and flung back her thick, shoulder-length hair with her free hand. In the evenings she untied it and brushed it loose over her shoulders. There were a few strands of grey amongst the auburn waves but she chose to ignore them, as she did the fine lines around her eyes. She was not vain and she had no idea how attractive she was as she neared her fifties, but she was comfortable with herself, physically and mentally, and it showed in her character. In jeans and low-heeled shoes she only reached Jack's shoulder. She had bought her shirt in Waghorn Stores in Newlyn Strand. It was a shop where anything could be purchased, from hardware to hard-wearing clothing, from crockery to gardening tools, from light bulbs to pet food, and if what you wanted wasn't on display they were sure to have it upstairs. The shirt was thick and heavy, checked in blue and black, and although the smallest size it was meant for a man and therefore swamped Rose's petite figure. She was out in all weathers for most of the year and her fashion sense was non-existent during the daytime. Over the shirt she wore a baggy sweater, streaked with paint and fraying at the hem, beneath which the tails of the shirt could be seen. To Jack Pearce she always looked vulnerable and desirable but, to his cost, he had learnt she was only the latter. She lifted her arms as if to display herself, being careful not to spill her drink. 'Well, as you can see, I'm fine. Why shouldn't I be?' She did not want to hear the answer.

'Because it was so unlike you, so completely out of character for you to panic and to act the way you did, if you don't mind me saying so.'

'But I do mind, Jack.' She smiled sardonically and sipped the wine, making a point of not offering him a drink. 'Are you here officially? Am I to be charged with anything?'

'Of course not. Mistakes happen. I just thought . . .'

Rose was already moving. She had placed her glass on the table and opened the side door. 'Goodnight, Jack. Thank you for calling.' His mouth dropped open in surprise. 'I said goodnight. Now go. I'll catch pneumonia standing here in this draught.'

With an angry shrug he thrust his hands into the pockets of his reefer jacket and stomped out of the house. Rose locked the door with a decisive twist of the key but her satisfaction didn't last. She slumped into a kitchen chair and played with the stem of the wine glass, which was cold between her fingers. It would have been the perfect opportunity to explain. Once his anger had abated Jack would have listened, she was sure of that. He had always believed and trusted her in the past. It was too late now, and she had no intention of telephoning him. An awful end to an awful day, she thought.

It had been one of those balmy days with which the area was often blessed in winter. Late October and most of November had been wet, heavy rain had been accompanied by gale force winds, then, just when it should have been getting colder, the temperature started to rise. Indian summer days were followed by spectacular sunsets and chilly evenings. It was difficult to believe Christmas was so close . . .

Thinking back over the events of that day led to nostalgic memories of her youth. Having left art college, Rose had arrived in Penzance at the age of twenty-one with no idea of what to expect. Her intention was to remain for six months whilst she studied the artists of the Newlyn School and did some painting herself. But fate had other things in store and she had never gone home. Lodgings had been organised before her arrival and she had soon settled down to work but, unable to sell many of the oils she completed, she had turned to watercolours. A chance meeting with Barry Rowe, the owner of a shop which sold greetings cards and postcards amongst other things, had altered the direction of her career. Needing a map, she had gone into the shop. Barry, noticing her sketchpad, politely asked if she was an artist. Rose had shown him some of her watercolours and before she knew it he had employed her on an almost full-time basis, using her designs on his notelets and cards. He had a printing works in Camborne where they were produced. Later Rose had taken up photography and sold much of her work to postcard manufacturers as well as taking portrait pictures. The oils, which she had so loved painting, had long gone by the wayside. Until recently, that is. Her new friends, met at a party thrown by Mike and Barbara Phillips, a couple she had known for many years, had given her so much encouragement that she was now relatively successful in marketing and selling her work. A single painting had done it, the one she had started immediately after David's death, one she could not recall finishing. Recovering it from its hiding place because she had an idea it might make a suitable gift for Mike's fiftieth birthday, she had been startled by how good it was. Anger and grief and experience had lent her work the maturity it had previously lacked and had added something which even she was unable to define. Mike and his guests had been genuinely impressed with her talent and things had continued from there.

Today she had gone back to capture the barren ruggedness of the countryside rather than the dramatic coastline or the prettiness of the villages which nestled in the coves. The work depicted the ruins of an old engine house at a disused mine. With the trees and the undergrowth still in autumnal colouring, it was the perfect place to test her ability in her new medium. Sitting there in the early afternoon, she had heard a scream: the high-pitched scream of a woman.

She rested her head in her hands. No, she had not imagined it. Superstitious and able to sense things almost as well as the Cornish could, she knew the difference between reality and fancy. Nor was it some trick of acoustics, the countryside was well known to her. She knew how many areas of open country could be dangerous with hidden and uncovered mine shafts which might suddenly subside. Still, she saw how it must appear and was annoyed to think that those who had answered her summons, made from the mobile phone she now carried with her, probably thought her an hysterical female. An ambulance and the cliff rescue team had turned up. At least they hadn't sent a helicopter from Culdrose as well. There was nothing she could do now but to put it from her mind and live with the humiliation: despite a thorough search no one had been found.

She glanced at the cooker clock. It was time to get changed. Nick Pascoe was taking her to a classical concert at the Methodist church in Chapel Street, and afterwards they were going for something to eat. This was to be their third meeting. So far they had done no more than to share a few drinks, once in Newlyn, and once in St Ives where Nick lived and worked.

Rose knew of his reputation as an artist both locally and nationally yet she had hardly noticed him at Barbara and Mike's party where they were introduced. This, she realised, was due to the excitement she had felt at the more than favourable reception of her painting which she had wrapped and presented to Mike. It showed a wild, storm-ridden coastline which reflected the state of her mind at the time she had worked on it. Only when he telephoned to invite her out did Nick's face come clearly to mind. It was a nice face, lined and rugged and weatherbeaten. His hair, completely grey, was the colour of her filing cabinet and he wore it brushed back from the forehead and long over the collar. His green eyes were peculiarly speckled and changed with the light. At the party he had worn jeans, a shirt and a denim jacket and, having seen him twice since, Rose wondered if he possessed any other clothes. Only the shirt had been different. On the first occasion it was black, worn over a black T-shirt; the second time it had been similar to the one she was now wearing herself. Mounting the stairs, she smiled as she imagined what her mother would have to say about him. 'Honestly, Rose, he might have put on a jacket and tie.' Rose's parents were conventional and were still bewildered by their artistic only child who had adopted the lifestyle and dress of her own kind.

Rose showered and washed her hair. Bending her head she flung the wet tresses forward over her face to give them more body as the drier buzzed noisily. From the wardrobe she took a black dirndl skirt with an embroidered hem and a silky green shirt. Over this she wore a black jacket. Shoes were a problem so she settled for her one good pair of boots in tan leather. At least they matched her handbag.

They had arranged to meet in the Admiral Benbow, a pub and restaurant in Chapel Street in Penzance. The drinking was done upstairs, at the long bar or in the room which overlooked the sea; the restaurant was on ground level, behind a door with a low lintel. The building dated back to the days of smugglers and a tunnel was supposed to run from the building to the sea. There were ancient beams and nautical artefacts and unmatching furniture made from heavy wood.

Rose had no intention of driving as she had already had a glass of wine and there would be more drinks with Nick, but thanks to Jack Pearce it was now too late to walk. She glanced at her watch. If she hurried she could catch the next bus; failing that it would mean a taxi. She was surprised to feel anxious that she might be late.

Just as Rose reached the nearest stop the lights of the bus appeared over the brow of the hill. She shivered, glad she had not had to wait. I'm soft now, she thought, recalling the weeks of snow and ice she had regularly endured as a child. The slightest drop in temperature and the inhabitants of West Penwith complained that it was freezing. However, she admitted, handing the driver the exact money, by local standards it was cold. She sat at the back of the small single-decker and unbundled her winter coat from beneath her. She did not want to crease it. It was a recent acquisition, pure wool in a rusty colour which, with her hair resting across her shoulders and the tan boots below, made her as autumnal in appearance as the countryside. Rose rarely bought new clothes. When she did, she looked after them excessively well for about three months then they received the same treatment as older items: they were thrown over the backs of chairs, dropped on to the bed or even left to slide off their hangers in the walk-in cupboard which served as a wardrobe.

She shifted again, trying to keep the material smooth, and caught the eye of a rheumy old man with a stick. She smiled but he turned away, clearing his throat and hawking into a tissue. Rose averted her eyes.

The bus lumbered down the hill and towards Penzance. Along the Promenade was a continuous string of plain lights which were now a permanent fixture. They went well with the new Victorian-type lamp-posts. The festive lights were already strung in Penzance and would be shining brightly. There were only two weeks until Christmas and she had made no plans. Other years, since David's death, her parents had arrived and taken over. Last year she had spent in the company of Jack Pearce. They had enjoyed a quiet day by themselves. Rose had cooked a joint and Jack had provided champagne, wine and whisky. In the evening Laura and Trevor had joined them and they had played cards and got merrily tipsy. There would be no Jack this year and she had persuaded her parents they were not to cancel their own plans.

Despite the distance between them, they kept in touch regularly by letter and telephone and knew their daughter well enough to understand that the past was behind her and that even if she was alone her memories could no longer make her sad. Laura Penfold, her best friend, had invited her for lunch but Rose would not dream of imposing when Laura's own family were coming to stay. 'They're arriving on Christmas Eve and leaving on the 27th,' Laura had said. 'Just right. Not long enough to try my patience.' Rose knew the Christmas Day procedure in the Penfold household: Laura would do all the preparations in advance but it was Trevor and their daughters-in-law who cooked the meal, allowing Laura to go to the pub with her three sons. They had all moved away, none having followed their father into fishing. Perhaps it's just as well with the way things are going, Rose thought, as the bus pulled in opposite the post office. She alighted and thanked the driver then crossed the road, stopping at the top of the street to glance in the window of Dorothy Perkins. Across the road a shaven-headed model stood in the window of a boutique. Posed with its legs wide apart, knees bent inwards and an aggressive grimace on its face, it caught Rose's attention. She stood back and studied it, wondering why ugliness could sometimes be appealing as well as eye-catching.

A vicious wind caught the hem of her coat and lifted her hair as she rounded the corner and made her way down Chapel Street to the Admiral Benbow. Upstairs in the bar Nick Pascoe was half seated on a tall stool, one foot on the ledge below the counter. A pint of beer stood in front of him. He rose as she approached, swept back his hair with his long, narrow fingers and leant over to kiss her cheek. Apart from shaking hands at Mike's birthday party it was the first tactile gesture on either side yet it felt perfectly natural. 'Wine?' he asked.

'Please. You're sure this starts at seven forty-five? There're people going in already.'

'Positive. Don't panic. I didn't think to book anywhere to eat, I'd forgotten about the Christmas party crowds.'

'Oh, we'll get in somewhere. It's Wednesday, it shouldn't be a problem.'

They sipped in silence for a few minutes. Nick made a roll-up and lit it, blowing smoke from the corner of his mouth. 'Rose, is something bothering you?'

'No!' She was astonished. It was astute of him to realise anything was wrong, but she had been trying to forget her earlier foolishness. There was no time to tell him now, maybe later, after the music had worked its magic. She checked the time. 'Ten minutes. Shall we walk over?'

Nick downed the last two inches of beer. He wore jeans again, his best pair, Rose assumed, as they weren't threadbare nor were they covered in paint splashes. Over them was a fisherman's jersey with the collar of a pale blue shirt poking over the top. He wore no jacket so probably had a T-shirt underneath as well. Rose blinked in surprise. She had been undressing him mentally.

Nick took her arm as they mounted the steps to the broad-fronted church, whose interior was more ornate than its outward appearance suggested. It was filled with the rustlings of programme sheets and muted conversation. Discreet coughing continued until the orchestra filed down the far aisle. The musicians took their places in front of the altar and began to tune their instruments.

Only once did Rose look at Nick. He had his eyes half closed as a Mozart piano concerto washed over them. This was followed by a movement from Beethoven's Second Symphony and then a soprano whose pure notes filled the church and made Rose shiver. The fourth piece was by a composer of whom Rose had not heard. To her ears the music sounded discordant and she wasn't sorry when the interval came. They left the church as Nick wanted a cigarette, then, giggling like teenagers, they dived over the road to the Turk's Head where they just managed to get a drink before it was time to return.

'Enjoy it?' Nick asked when the concert was over.

'It was lovely. I should make the effort more often. There're so many things going on if you bother to look. I usually get to see one of the male voice choirs every month or so, though.'

'Ah, you can't beat hearing Cornishmen sing. Can you sing, Rose?'

'Not a note.'

They were heading up the hill along with many of the audience who would be making for one of the car-parks. 'Where're we going?'

Rose shrugged. 'Chinese as we're up here now?'

They decided upon the nearer of the two almost adjacent restaurants, both situated on the first floor above other premises. It was surprisingly busy but they were given a window seat. 'So, let's hear it. What has upset my painter in oils?' Nick asked, having recalled his earlier impression of Rose's strange mood.

Unsure of the significance of the possessive pronoun – was he making fun of her because she was only just finding her feet whereas he had been established for years, or was it a sign of affection? – she felt awkward and almost kept her counsel. But knowing how the grapevine worked he would hear within a short time anyway. Feeling the heat in her face, Rose said, 'I did something incredibly stupid. I was so . . . Ah, well. I must've been wrong.'

Nick was sitting back in his chair with his arms folded. He raised a hand and rested his index finger against his lips. 'And from that short garbled paragraph, the penultimate sentence, if you don't mind me pointing out, lacking a complete predicate, I'm supposed to deduce exactly what piece of stupidity you have been engaged in.'

Rose smiled. He *was* making fun of her now. 'All right, I'll explain. I was out painting. I heard a scream. It came from near an old mine shaft. I went to investigate. I heard a second scream. I ran back to the car and rang the police from my mobile phone. The emergency services turned up in force.' She shrugged. 'They didn't find anyone.'

'Most comprehensible, and not a sub-clause anywhere.'

'Pedant.' Rose was playing with her chopsticks as the waiter arrived with the wine Nick had ordered. She opened the menu and studied it, choosing her main dish immediately because she knew that if she hesitated she would keep changing her mind.

'Seriously, though, if you did hear a scream you did the right thing. I didn't know you had a mobile phone,' He raised an eyebrow but Rose did not take the hint and give him the number. Nick placed a hand over hers but only to stop her fiddling. He removed it as soon as he saw the closed expression on her face.

'No. Well, I mostly forget to take it out with me.' As with the time-operated light in her hall, it was Jack who had suggested she got one.

'It was handy today.'

Rose snorted. 'Handy to have everyone arrive a bit sooner, that's all.'

'Yes, but when you're out by yourself at night, it's safer.'

Rose chewed the side of her mouth. He was right, of course. The West Country, for so long always a step behind and a reminder of a more gentle age, was now no stranger to crime and seemed to be catching up with everywhere else. 'So, I'm walking up Causewayhead and about to be mugged or attacked and I say, "Hold on a minute while I get out my phone to ring the police"?'

'Now who's being pedantic? You know perfectly well what I mean.'

'Well, it's heavy, I could always use it as a cosh.'

Nick shook his head, smiling as the waiter brought several dishes and arranged them on the hotplates. Nick indicated that Rose should begin before he helped himself to food. Having tasted it he nodded approvingly then continued, 'It could've been the wind.'

'No. I can't expect you to believe me but it was a scream. A woman's scream. Oh, let's forget it, it's one of those things that happen round here, that'll never be understood.'

'Did anyone know where you were going today?'

'What difference would that have made?' Rose, her carefully loaded chopsticks halfway to her mouth, felt a fleeting panic.

There was a strange expression on his face as he said, 'I'm not sure.' He paused. 'I just wondered.'

'I told Stella and Daniel. In fact, I think it was Stella who originally suggested the scene. I'm so grateful to them, Nick, they've really taken me under their wing. They're all so nice. I expected, well, I'm not sure, not jealousy, I'm nowhere in their league, but perhaps resentment at a new face amongst the recognised.'

'We're not like that, Rose. I'm surprised you should have thought so.'

'I apologise, I meant no offence. It's just that after coping on my own for so long and allowing myself to settle for second best . . .' She shrugged again and pushed her hair back over her shoulders, tucking it neatly behind her ears so as not to get it in the way of the food as she leant over the bowl.

Nick remained silent. He guessed wrongly that she had been suffering from a lack of confidence. Having lost the husband she had loved deeply and with whom she had been so happy that her talent had taken second place, she must have needed courage to change direction so late in life. He was annoyed for having underestimated her. It had been easy for him, he had been one of the lucky ones, his work had been shown and bought almost from the beginning. Unlike Rose he had not married, although there had been several long-standing relationships. The last one had ended six months ago. Jenny was an artist's model, one of those wild-looking creatures with olive skin and a tangle of black hair and eyes that could seduce with a glance. Nature, he thought, could be very deceptive. Jenny had wanted nothing more than to settle down and have babies and she had believed Nick would oblige on this score. After three years she had flung her few possessions into a bag and walked out, slamming the door, shouting recriminations about her wasted youth and his having used her. Initially too stunned to retaliate, Nick had remained standing in the kitchen, spatula in hand, and continued to fry the mackerel that was to have been their supper. Used? he had thought. She lives with me free of charge, off my earnings, and eats my food which I generally end up cooking. If she'd got out the hoover once in a while it might have helped.

He had flung down his cooking implements and rushed to the door. 'Used?' he bellowed down the narrow alley from the cottage door, much to the astonishment of locals and holidaymakers alike – although the latter had probably lapped it up as a piece of local colour. 'Who's used who, I wonder?' But Jenny had already disappeared around the corner.

Rose was completely different. She was lovely but more mature, she had known pain and had learnt to deal with it and he admired what little he had seen of her work. He sensed that she would not play games, that whatever occurred between them she would be straight with him. That would make a change from Jenny's prevarications. And, he realised, as he watched her picking expertly at the dishes with her chopsticks, she did not feel the need to talk constantly.

'What?' Rose looked up just in time to catch his grin.

'You're enjoying that.'

'I am.'

There was no way he was going to say he had also been thinking how much he desired her. But were these things enough? And why was he even thinking them? It was far too soon to tell how or if the relationship would develop. At least he would like her as a friend, if nothing else.

'I'm going to Stella's exhibition tomorrow. It's the opening, she invited me.'

'Then you'd better not drive. She'll press wine on you till it's coming out of your ears.'

'Doesn't sound like much of a hardship to me.'

'Wait and see.'

'I can't say I've noticed she drinks a lot.'

'No, that's the point. She doesn't. It's nerves.'

'Stella?'

'I know. Hard to credit. But it's the same every time she has a new show. She's always terrified each one'll be the last.'

'Right now I'd settle for one.'

'Then you'll need more canvases. How many have you done now?'

'Oh, several decent ones. It's odd, the ones I liked least have sold. You're grinning again. What is it this time?'

'You're learning. You're beginning to recognise what's good and what isn't. How do you tell?'

Rose frowned. 'I don't know. It's just a feeling.'

'Then you're probably right. Can you finish this?' Nick indicated the beef in black bean sauce.

'No, I think we over-ordered.' There was still a dish of spare ribs hardly touched.

'Shall I get the bill?'

'Yes. Look at the time, it's almost eleven-thirty. We'll split it.'

'I wouldn't dream of it.' This was definitely not something Jenny would have offered to do. Another plus point to Rose Trevelyan.

The waiter arrived to clear their dishes. 'Do you think you could put the ribs in a take-away container, please?'

Across the table Nick's jaw dropped. 'Have you got a dog?'

'No, they're for me, unless you want them.'

His laughter caused heads to turn. 'Do you ever waste anything?'

'Not if I can help it. Besides, if I wake in the night I'm always hungry.'

'You eat them cold?'

'I do. You should try it sometime.' She pursed her mouth in amusement. 'I have other habits you might find disgusting.'

'Please, spare me them tonight. Let's get your coat. Taxi home or shall I walk you?'

'A taxi, it's miles out of your way.' Rose stopped, her arms half in the sleeves of her coat. 'How will you get home?'

'I'm staying with a friend in Penzance.'

'Oh, I see.'

The waiter rang for a taxi and they stood in the doorway at the bottom of the stairs out of the wind until it arrived. Clutching the tinfoil container of ribs, Rose was thinking about his throw-away comment. Had he already arranged to stay with this friend or had he been expecting to go home with her? He had offered to walk her back. Too late now for speculation, she thought as the familiar shape of a Stone's taxi hove into view. Nick opened the back door then felt silly as she got into the front passenger seat and greeted the driver by name. 'Thanks. I really enjoyed this evening,' she said, winding down the window. 'My treat next time.' Then, wishing she had not been so forward, she asked the driver to take her home.

She walked up the steep path which led directly to the side door of the house, which was set into the cliffside. To reach the front door she would have had to turn right and pick her way in the dark along the uneven path, alongside which overgrown shrubs sloped down to the road. Like her friends, Rose rarely used this door and after the last heavy rain she discovered that the wood had swollen. Letting herself into the kitchen, she was thinking what a strange sort of day it had been. Still that lingering cry echoed in her head. Perhaps she was going mad or her imagination had been working overtime, although she could not recall thinking about anything other than her work when she had heard that eerie sound. The embarrassment lingered and Jack Pearce's reminder had been unnecessary. And what had Nick said about anyone knowing where she was? What on earth had he meant by that? Was there someone who wanted to scare her or make her look a fool?

Too tired to care, she went upstairs and got ready for bed, taking one last look at the bay and the lights of Newlyn harbour below. The moon was partially obscured by a cloud but there was still light enough to undress by. No one could see in: passing cars or the unlikely pedestrian at that time of night would be too low down beneath the overhang of her garden and any seaman would need a high-powered telescope. if they had a sudden desire to watch a middle-aged widow undressing.

Rose was wary about returning to the mine but more work was required on the painting. Stella had seen it in its early stages and had confirmed Rose's own opinion that it was good. She could not abandon it because of some imagined noise but there would not be time tomorrow. Laura, whom she had been neglecting, was coming for coffee and there was Stella's preview in the evening. There were also a few things she needed to do in Penzance.

There was Maddy, too, another of the St Ives crowd, whom Rose felt she would like to know better. She sensed they shared something in common, something deeper than mutual acquaintances although she had not yet worked out what. Madeleine Duke was self-supporting and could turn her hand to many things. She made ceramics and pottery and was skilful at textile printing, and she sold her goods from a little shop in a back lane in which she worked as she waited for custom. She had placed a small sign on the street corner, propped against one of the tiny cottages which made up the village of St Ives. Rose had to admit that it was a beautiful place. The sand was fine, the colour of clotted cream, and the sea, beloved by surfers, was bluer than the Aegean. If you arrived by train the breath-taking view was framed by a fringe of palm trees at the side of the line. But to live there was another matter. Unable to move for tourists in the summer, Rose would have felt claustrophobic. St Ives had its fishing history but Newlyn was still very much a working village, no quaintness unless you knew where to look for it, nothing but the concrete edifice of the fish market and the ice factories. Most visitors drove straight through on their way to the picturesque village of Mousehole.

There was at least another half-hour until daylight when Rose opened her eyes at seven. Switching on the bedside lamp she pulled on the towelling robe she used as a dressing gown in the winter, tied the belt and went downstairs, shivering. Something must be wrong with the heating. It was timed to come on at six and although it was set at a temperature low enough only to take the chill off the air, it was missed that morning. She opened the door off the kitchen which led into what had once been the larder or pantry but now served as a laundry and store-room. The light had gone out on the boiler.

'Damn it.' Rapidly losing patience, she saw that it needed more skill than she possessed to get it to work again. Laura's husband, Trevor, was home from sea and there was little in the way of engines or appliances that baffled him. She'd ring before Laura came and see if he could help her out. Meanwhile coffee was needed. Filter coffee, she decided. Whilst it was running through the machine she went into the lounge and knelt in front of the grate. There were a few embers beneath the ashes of the logs – with a bit of luck she could get the fire going quickly. Stuffing newspaper concertinas in its midst and adding a few bits of driftwood which she had picked up from the beach and which burned so well and so brightly because they were seasoned and salty, she lit a match. The flames caught immediately. Adding a few lumps of coal she waited until they, too, caught then balanced a dry log on top. Sitting back on her heels she felt the heat on her face as she listened to the snapping and hissing of kindling and solid fuel while the sparks flew up the chimney.

Outside the sky was clear, the last of the stars less brilliant as dawn approached. The moon had set an hour ago. The hydrangea bushes with their spiky twigs were bare but had borne new shoots since October and, she had read, there were camellias flowering in a nearby country house garden. As if to prove the clemency of the weather there was a jug of narcissi, flown over from Scilly, on the mantelpiece and the first daffodils would soon be appearing in bud in the shops of Penzance. There was no hint of a frost. It probably wasn't much colder outside than inside the house at the moment. Bank, post office, library, hairdresser's, she reminded herself. A twice-yearly trim was something she endured rather than enjoyed.

Sporadic spluttering from the kitchen told her that the coffee was ready. It was rich and strong and just as she liked it. Gratefully she sipped the first mouthful, her hands clasped around the mug for warmth. Thankfully the immersion heater was independent of the boiler and she was able to have a bath.

In jeans and shirt and a heavy knitted sweater, she found some old woollen socks which had holes in the toes but were nonetheless warm and put them on before stuffing her feet into the leather hiking boots she wore for most of the winter. Not only were they comfortable but they were a necessity as her outdoor work often took her over rough terrain.

At eight-thirty she dialled Laura's number and was answered by a yawning female voice.

'Did I wake you?' Laura was usually an early riser.

'No, I was up, but we didn't get to bed until two. We had some friends over and – you know how it is. How did it go, with Nick? He's not there, is he?'

'No, Laura, he isn't here,' Rose said firmly. 'Nor was he last night.'

'Don't get teasy, you know I have to know. Why're you ringing, can't you make it this morning?'

'Actually, I need a favour. Is Trevor busy today?'

'If you call lying about with the newspaper before

wandering off to the Star for a lunchtime drink busy, then yes, he is. What's the problem? Surely not the car?'

'No. The central heating boiler.' The car was relatively new, bought with a legacy of a thousand pounds an old friend had left her. It had replaced the yellow Mini which had been a gift from David and which she had hung on to for far too long for sentimental reasons. Now she was the proud owner of a blue Metro which started first time and had only had three previous owners. Mike Phillips had gone with her to choose it, claiming he knew about such matters. It seemed he did – doctor or no doctor, he had proved he knew almost as much about the internal workings of the combustion engine as he did about the patients upon whom he wielded his scalpel.

'No problem, I'll bring him with me. See you later.'

Rose hung up. She had known Laura since they were in their early twenties but it felt as if they had always known one another. There were times when Laura would preface a remark with something along the lines of 'Remember Miss so-and-so who taught us in the third year?' or quote the name of a school-friend as if they had actually been to school together. Laura had never left Newlyn and had vowed that she never would. Before marrying Trevor she had travelled but she had always been glad to return. It had shocked her when her boys, one by one, had moved away.

Rose had finally been accepted. She had, after all, married a Cornishman and kept his name and she had not tried to impress but had made a slow integration into the community. Doreen Clarke, a more recent friend, once told her, 'You'm all right, maid, you don't give yourself no airs and graces like they London people.'

Rose did not bother to explain that she came from Gloucestershire and had lived in the middle of nowhere, surrounded only by verdant English countryside and cows and sheep, and that trips into Swindon or Cheltenham were a rare treat. Her father had been a country farmer who had lived through the good times before BSE and European intervention; he had hunted with hounds and had, so her mother told her, been on a protest rally against the anti-hunting campaign. Rose found it hard to believe that her conventional, rather self-effacing father had put himself so much in the limelight. He had retired whilst still in his fifties and sold the farm. He and his wife had then bought a small stone cottage with a manageable garden and spent the intervening years doing all the things they had not had time for before. Rose saw the problems other people her age had with elderly parents who were frail or senile and knew she was lucky. On the other hand she suspected a lot of it was to do with their attitude. They did not believe themselves to be old or incapable of doing anything they chose. There was, she had long ago realised, no point in discussing her past at all with Doreen, who would not recognise the difference between London and the Gloucestershire countryside because anyone from across the Tamar was 'one of they' and therefore a Londoner.

As Rose loaded the washing machine, changed the bed and tidied up, the sun came up, a wintry yellow but promising another fine day. She finished some paperwork until the washing machine had ended its cycle then piled the clothes into a basket and took them outside to hang on the line she had strung from the shed to the highest branch of a tree. Towels flapped in the breeze coming off the sea, an easterly breeze, she noticed, no wonder it was colder.

The shed at the back of the garden had been cleared out and the rubbish taken to the dump. Anything serviceable she had given to the charity shops in Penzance. With a Calor gas heater installed and the door and windows made draught-proof, it was where she had recently taken to working if the light was right. At other times, if she wasn't painting in the open air, she used the attic which she had had converted many years previously. One half had been partitioned off to use as a dark-room for her photography work, although it was little used lately, and the other half with the sloping window in the roof was perfect for colouring her sketches as it was at the side of the house and therefore faced north.

The last item of clothing had been pegged firmly to the line just as she heard the familiar voices of Trevor and Laura, who had arrived on foot. Their faces were pink and they were both in heavy jackets. Laura, despite her height and thinness, was typically Cornish in appearance. She possessed deep, dark eyes and naturally rosy cheeks and her long dark hair, loose today, flew about her face in untidy clumps. She had never been able to control the natural wave. Trevor was an inch shorter than his wife, his face weathered with lines radiating from his brown eyes. His hair, too, curled and was worn long although of a lighter brown than Laura's. Through the beard he had not shaved off in all the years that Rose had known him, his lips were red and full. A tiny silver cross dangled from his left ear.

'What've you broken this time, Rose?' were his words of greeting.

'The boiler won't light. It just went out. I didn't touch it,' she added defensively although she had fiddled with it that morning.

'I'll take a look.' With the familiarity of an old friend Trevor let himself into the house and went straight to the boiler and removed its cover. The two women followed. Rose shut the door and put the washing basket on the draining board before getting out milk and sugar. She reached for the tin of biscuits she kept for guests, knowing that Trevor would eat some. Laura, too, had no mean appetite but she never gained an ounce of weight. Rose was also naturally slender but tended not to eat at all at stressful times.

There was a whoosh from the laundry room. Rose and Laura exchanged a complicit glance. Trevor had fixed it. Water gurgled in the radiators and just the sound of it made Rose feel warmer. 'A well-earned coffee,' she said, handing him a heavily sweetened mugful. 'Do you want more milk?' Trevor shook his head. The job had only taken minutes but over the years Rose had learnt that Trevor was offended if she offered remuneration. Instead she repaid him with a packet of tobacco or a few cans of his favourite beer.

He sat at the table and got out the makings of a roll-up, scattering tobacco as he did so. Not a man for conversation unless it was necessary, he left the talking to the women. Years at sea had taught him to keep his own counsel. Cooped up in a confined space with a crew from whom there was no escape until you landed had made many a man taciturn. He listened, all the same, and took in all he heard.

'Rose,' he said, licking the adhesive strip of his cigarette paper and dextrously twisting it around the tobacco, 'what happened yesterday?' He looked into her face with his shrewd brown eyes.

She sighed. 'You might as well hear it from me as from anyone.' The explanation already sounded tired to her own ears.

'That's just about how I heard it.' Trevor inhaled and blew out smoke with his eyes half closed.

'You didn't say anything to me, Trevor.' Laura was indignant. She flung back her hair as if she had suffered the worst possible affront. Not knowing things, for Laura, was unbearable and for her husband to withhold information was an unthinkable insult.

'No. Not till I heard it from the source. Strange goings-on, that. Where was this?'

Rose told him. Trevor shook his head. 'It was no echo then.'

'No.' Rose wished everyone would stop discussing it, but only because she was still convinced that what she had heard was real. However, the area had been searched thoroughly, and she could only question her sanity.

Trevor crossed his legs and folded his arms, one hand with the cigarette hovering over the ashtray Rose had placed before him. 'You might be artistic, but I wouldn't call you sensitive or fanciful. If it wasn't an echo or a trick of the wind and no one was found, then there still has to be an explanation.'

Rose was later to recall those words and to see that she

35

ought to have made more of them. 'That's just it, Trevor, but I can't come up with an answer. At least you know me well enough to realise I believed what I heard at the time.'

He shook his head and the wavy hair moved with it. 'The way I see it is like this, if you're not breaking things you're landing yourself in trouble. Were you accident-prone as a cheel?'

Rose slapped his arm affectionately, knowing he was sending her up. 'No. I've never even broken a bone.'

'Well, mind you don't now. Take my advice and keep away from they places. If you're right, and I'm not saying I disbelieve you, then there'll be trouble in it for you somewhere along the line. You know what you're like, Rose Trevelyan.'

What he said made sense but she had no intention of letting her friends know that she planned to return to the mine tomorrow. That painting was good, too good to relinquish now, she had to finish it. Pouring more coffee, she listened to Laura's plans for Christmas.

'Are you sure you won't come to us? You know we'd love to have you. Besides, it'll be such a houseful one more won't matter, and the boys worship you.'

That was, Rose thought, putting it a bit strongly, but she did get on well with them.

'Come on, girl, if you want a hand with the shopping.' Trevor stood up. Like many local families they did not possess a car. If the men were at sea they didn't travel far when they returned home and there were ample buses into Penzance and from there to other places. There were also enough people who did have transport and who were prepared to offer lifts. They walked down the path in single file and waved before disappearing from view.

Rose knew that many villages and small towns comprised the same mix of pubs and small shops which served the locals, but in Newlyn there was a difference. It was in both the people themselves and the one thing which bound them together: the sea. The sea and its produce and the dangers it held, proven by the tragedies which, when they occurred, affected not one person but many in such a close-knit community.

She rinsed the mugs and inverted them on the draining board before glancing at the sky, which could change in seconds. There were still no clouds. She slipped on a jacket, picked up her large leather handbag and went outside. The walk along the sea front would do her good and she could change her library books on the way up to Penzance. Breathing in the clean air, she made her way down the hill, waving to a fish buyer as she passed the market. It was busy but the auctioneer's voice could be heard above the clattering of fish boxes.

Library, bank, post office, hairdresser's, she reminded herself again as she reached the level surface of Newlyn Green.

# CHAPTER TWO

Stella Jackson paced the honey-coloured, highly polished sanded boards of her living room floor, cigarette in hand. Daniel Wright, her husband, ignored her. He was used to the first night nerves from which she suffered as much in St Ives as in one of the big London galleries. And tonight they were to be honoured by the presence of a well-known art dealer. Daniel was not alone in adrniring his wife's work as well as the woman herself and was therefore unable to understand her insecurity. It was some years now since he had stopped trying to reassure her; this anxiety was part of her, something which she had to endure and which, he realised, helped her artistically. If she lost the desire to improve, to be the best, if she took her talent for granted, it might slide into mediocrity. In many ways they were worlds apart but their marriage worked and they allowed one another plenty of freedom.

Daniel had been commissioned to produce a sculpture for the gardens of a government property in London. Twice he had travelled up with plans and then the model from which he would work. It was now under way. The basic shape had been formed and sat in his studio wrapped in damp cloths. It would take months to complete and he couldn't afford a mistake. Some days he didn't touch it at all but merely stared at the plans and his initial drawing. Then he would run his hands over the clay. When he could feel in his fingertips the form which would finally emerge and picture it as well as he knew his own body, then he would continue. For now he was happy enough to offer whatever support he could to Stella at the private viewing of her exhibition.

The flat over her gallery in St Ives had once been a net loft. They had moved there from Zennor five years previously, although Daniel still preferred the old granite house despite its relative inconvenience. The loft had been partially renovated before they moved in but they had decided to leave the rafters in their original form rather than build a ceiling. They sloped up to the roof, forming an apex and creating a sense of spaciousness. The decor appeared very casual but the effect had taken Stella a long time to achieve as she searched for just the right material for cushions and curtains and the rugs that were thrown over the settees. The television and video recorder were hidden in a cupboard built into the wall, as was their collection of CDs and the player. Against the longest wall was a dining table made of oak, with matching chairs. It was second-hand but had cost more than the modern equivalent they had looked at. Basic wooden shelving, made by Daniel, held their numerous books. At the bottom were the heavier, glossy tomes containing pictures of the great works of artists and sculptors. Above were dictionaries and reference books, while the top three shelves held novels. It was an eclectic collection. Many of the paperbacks were Penguins with their original covers and priced at half a crown or less. The edges of the pages were orange with age and the books still retained the smell peculiar to the roughish paper on which they were printed.

The kitchen was small and adjoined this room. It was extremely functional, space being at a premium, and had been designed by a seafaring friend who had worked within the limitations of a ship's galley. The bedroom and bathroom had not required much improvement; the latter some modernisation, the former only redecoration. The previous occupants, who had carried out the initial conversion, had had their main rooms downstairs.

The gallery ran the length and breadth of the building with only a small cubicle blocked off for office work and a kitchenette alongside it. A selection of Stella's new paintings, carefully framed and kept from the public eye, were now hanging on the walls and the six-foot removable partitions she had erected down the centre. Daniel had placed an order with the wine merchant, hired glasses and made sure there was at least one spare corkscrew and some whisky for those who didn't drink wine. There were also soft drinks and plates of food which were covered in foil and waiting in the fridge. There had been produced by Julie Trevaskith, the daughter of Molly who did their cleaning. Julie was at Cornwall College learning the catering trade. To earn some spending money she helped out in the gallery during the holidays.

'Want to go for a walk, burn off some of that nervous

energy?' Daniel asked, irritated by her restless pacing.

'No.' Stella shook her head, causing the straight black hair, cut to chin length, to swing. It looked unnatural, it was as dark as a string of jet beads except for a shock of grey springing from the crown. She was lean and willowy and dressed mainly in black but always with some splash of brilliance. Today, over the black ski-pants and satin tunic top she had slung a shawl of scarlet and emerald. The green was reflected in the huge earrings which dangled against her neck. She looked at Daniel and smiled. 'I know you're doing your best, I can't help it.'

He smiled back, wondering how a woman with slightly crooked teeth and a bit of a squint could be so sexy. Apart from her lissom body, there was something about her face which made men look twice. Maybe it was the bone structure or the fact that the two flaws, if they could be so called, cancelled each other out. It did not matter that her breasts were small, the whole effect added up to a beauty similar to that of a panther. Daniel wanted to take her to bed right then but she was too uptight to contemplate an act which might actually relieve her tension.

'I've asked a few people for drinks before we officially open.'

He liked the way she said 'we' although it was her gallery and her work on show. He tended to exclude her from his own artistic efforts, not letting her see anything until it was finished. Stella was far better at sharing than himself. 'Who's coming?'

'Maddy, Jenny, Barbara and Mike and Rose.' She counted them off on her fingers.

'No Nick?'

'He can't make it until later.' Stella smiled her feline smile. 'I didn't tell Rose he was coming.'

'She'll know, won't she? I thought they were seeing each other.'

'They are, as you put it, seeing each other, but I think that's as far as it goes. Don't start match-making.' She pointed a slender finger at him. Like the other seven it was bedecked with heavy silver rings and her nails, long and carefully filed, were scarlet, without a chip, the polish gleaming beneath its coat of clear varnish. No one would realise it had taken her an age to remove the paint from her hands and nails and wrists. Her lips, in the same shade, were pursed as she recalled it was Daniel who had paired Jenny off with Nick and that had turned out to be a disaster. It was now far enough in the past that it was safe to have them under the same roof.

'I won't. Cross my heart.' He did so as he stood up and stretched. 'Ought I to change?' He looked down at his brown cords. The nap on the knees had disappeared but his Viyella shirt with its tiny brown and white checks was perfectly presentable as was the matching brown V-necked sweater.

'You know I don't mind.'

'I think I will, trousers, anyway. You look so smart.'

She turned to hide a smile. Stella knew that had she insisted he tidy up he would have refused, stating that people must take him as he was.

'Hey, take it easy.' He patted her shoulder. Stella had jumped when the door bell chimed.

'Someone's early.' Brushing the cold metal of the rail with her hand she went down the circular wrought-iron staircase to see who it was. 'Jenny! It's unlike you to be so punctual.'

'I was hoping Maddy would be here. She's always the first to turn up.'

'Maddy? No, you're the first. You should've called for her on the way.'

Jenny put on her helpless face, her head on one side. 'I need a job.' She still modelled for artists, clothed or unclothed, having the sort of looks which transposed well to canvas, but it was by no means a full-time job and many couldn't afford to pay her at all. Sometimes she was rewarded with a meal or a painting that didn't sell or a few drinks in one of the pubs.

'Well, I don't see how Maddy can help. Oh, come on up. You look as if you could do with a drink. I certainly could but I promised myself I wouldn't start until someone arrived.'

Jenny smiled behind her back, knowing the state her hostess needed to work herself up into before she could begin to enjoy the evening. 'I just thought she might like someone to work in the shop. She could spend all her time at her craftwork then.'

'Be realistic, Jenny. All right, she's doing okay in the run-up to Christmas, but January and February? Even in the summer she just scrapes by.'

'I know. But I'm desperate, anything's worth a try. I don't suppose you . . .'

Stella raised her hands, palms facing forward. Her face

was stern. 'No chance, Jenny. Sorry.' Stella could have afforded to employ the girl but for some reason, when Jenny was involved, there was always trouble. She wasn't dishonest or rude, she was just one of those people who was always caught in the vortex of other people's problems and managed to exacerbate them. But Stella was honest enough to admit that the main reason was that Jenny Manders found it difficult to keep her hands off other women's men. The door bell rang again. 'You'll have to help yourself. On the side there.' Stella indicated the drinks that were kept for their personal use before clattering down the stairs to admit Mike and Barbara Phillips and Rose whose cars had converged in the car-park simultaneously.

Stella frowned. 'Barbara, you know Jenny, don't you?' Her life was hectic and there were occasions when she couldn't remember which of her friends and acquaintances already knew each other.

'Yes. Nice to see you again.'

Rose grinned at Jenny and accepted a glass of wine. Two would have to be her limit as she had come in the car. She knew nothing of Nick's three-year affair with Jenny, only that there had been someone until six months ago. These were new friends, more personal details had not yet been exchanged, although the basics of their lives were no secret.

'Ah, here already.' Daniel had changed and shaved. He greeted their guests whilst keeping an eye on Stella who was now chain-smoking. He liked the Phillips. Mike was a surgeon at Treliske hospital in Truro and his wife worked there as a physiotherapist. Rose Trevelyan was another woman he admired, and not only for her looks. She was a survivor. He wondered how Stella would fare if she did not have his constant support.

Maddy was the last to arrive. Her accent instantly placed her as an 'outsider', as someone from the Home Counties who had moved to Cornwall in search of the simple life, where she believed her dreamy manner and craftwork would be more appreciated. Having arrived only three years ago she was still considered to be an outsider, although she had made friends amongst the locals. Barbara, never less than elegant, smiled at Maddy's chosen ensemble. Over thick black tights she wore brown lace-up boots and a billowing smock in royal blue with embroidery across the tight-fitting chestband which flattened her curves. Beneath the smock was a striped T-shirt in olive green and white, over it a quilted jacket in squares of differing colours. On her head was a Paddington Bear hat with a large red flower stitched to the side. Long hair cloaked her shoulders. It was fair with a slight wave but of the dryish texture which did not shine even when newly washed. She resembled a character in a nursery rhyme.

Stella, a cigarette balanced in the corner of her mouth, replenished their drinks. Rose put her hand over her glass. 'Not for me, thanks.'

'Sure? Okay. I'm beginning to feel better already, Rose. You wouldn't believe what these evenings do to me.'

Rose nodded. Stella didn't know how lucky she was to be hosting one. Turning to speak to Barbara and Mike, acquaintances once, then firm friends from the start of David's illness when Mike had been his consultant and Rose's confidant, she studied Maddy Duke. Rose had met her at Stella's on several occasions and had found her to be amusing company, if a little zany, but beneath her cheerful exterior Rose guessed there was hidden pain.

Daniel circulated with the wine bottles but Rose told him she was saving her rationed second glass for the official opening.

'How's it going?' Mike Phillips, in causal trousers, shirt and sweater, finally got a chance to speak to Rose. He looked tired.

'I'm fine.'

'I can see you're fine, I meant the painting. Your oil has pride of place in our lounge. Did Barbara tell you?'

'No. I'm flattered.'

'How typical. We're the ones who're flattered. We had no idea you were that good.'

'Hidden talent,' Maddy said, joining them with a glass containing what appeared to be neat Scotch. 'I bet we don't know of half the local painters with hidden talents.'

'We?' Jenny had joined them. By her tone it was obvious she resented Maddy counting herself as one of them.

'I do think of myself as local, you know. I felt at home from the minute I came here.'

Rose sensed an animosity which she had not noticed between the two women before.

Jenny chewed the inside of her lip but said nothing. Instead she played with her thick black hair, which hung around her face like a frame. Her skin was good and her eyes were large and luminescent but it was her mouth which attracted. Full and pink, it hinted at both innocence and sensuality. She was about to move away and speak to Stella when Maddy asked Rose how Nick was. Jenny hesitated, her shoulders stiff. Rose replied that she had no reason to suppose he was other than well, but she had seen the give-away gesture and guessed that there had once been something between Nick and Jenny – and still might be, she thought, not liking the feeling this produced although she and Nick were no more than friends and there was certainly no commitment on either side. She decided to ignore her feelings and enjoy the rest of the evening although she continued to be aware of the vaguely hostile undercurrents in the room.

A few minutes later they all went downstairs and Stella unlocked the door. Guests were by invitation only. Stella stood at the front to welcome them into the brilliantly lit showroom whose lights now spilt out into the blackness of the narrow street. Earlier Stella had hurried her friends through the darkened gallery, allowing them no chance to glimpse her work.

Daniel went to the back to open the wine for Julie who had just arrived and had begun to take the foil off the trays of food. This was Stella's night, she must be allowed to enjoy the credit due to her whilst he and Julie handed around the food and drinks.

Spotlights had been switched on and the early arrivals, glasses in hand, wandered around admiring the paintings. Rose stopped in front of one she particularly liked. If only, she thought, almost able to feel and see the waves as they crashed over the headland.

'You will.' Stella, having silently positioned herself behind Rose, seemed to have read her mind. Ash from her cigarette sprinkled the front of Rose's blouse as Stella placed an arm across her shoulder. 'It's in you. Really it is. Of course there's a long way to go yet, and a lot of hard work in store for you. It isn't that easy to make it to the top.'

Rose nodded. Could it be possible that one day she would be in Stella's position? She was about to answer when she saw Nick's lanky figure duck through the doorway. He came straight over to her and Rose was glad there was a partition between her and Maddy and Jenny who were in conversation on the other side of it. His face lit up. 'I didn't say I was coming because I wasn't sure I could make it. Once you said you'd be here I had to come.'

'She's good, isn't she?' Rose ignored the compliment because there was a sudden silence on the other side of the partition.

'Better than she realises. You like this one?'

'Very much.' Rose accepted her second drink and took a canape from one of the trays Julie was handing around.

'How're you getting home?' Nick didn't seem at all interested in the exhibition but he had probably attended so many, including his own, that it wasn't much of a thrill for him.

'I've got the car.'

'Ah. Never mind. Are you all right? After yesterday, I mean?'

'Yes. Must've been my imagination.' She paused, and was unsure what then made her blurt out, 'I'm going back tomorrow if the weather's fine. I really want to finish that painting.'

'Yes, you must,' Stella insisted, having heard the last remarks as she approached them.

Rose moved away, intent on seeing the rest of Stella's new work. Nick followed, knowing that two pairs of eyes were on their backs.

Rose stopped to admire a small canvas, as yet unframed. It was an amusing piece showing a half-naked woman of a certain age; a little raddled, a little overweight but, judging from the smirk on her Picasso-style face, completely uncaring as she painted her own portrait from a full-length mirror. Rose wondered whether Stella intended it to make a statement or whether it was a work of pure fun. Her own smile faded as she overheard Jenny's words.

'Oh, there's no doubt about it, he'll have to take me back. How can he not? I am his responsibility, after all.'

'Is that what you *really* want?' Maddy asked, her voice clipped. 'Think about it, Jenny. You're the one who's always saying there's no going back. And there's . . . well, there's you know who to contend with.'

Rose felt suffocated and wanted to leave. With a determined stride she went out to the little kitchen and placed her glass on the fridge and her paper plate and serviette in the bin-liner put there for the rubbish, before returning to thank Stella and Daniel for inviting her.

With what she hoped was a cheerful wave to the others she walked out of the shop and straight back to the car. He's making a fool of me, she thought. And for the first time since she had met them Rose felt that maybe she didn't fit in with these exotic people after all, that there were things about them she didn't understand, and that she had no desire to join in their sexual games. For a moment she felt a pang for the faithful, reliable Barry Rowe who had yearned for her since before she had met David but who could never be more than a friend. Like Laura, he had been neglected lately and Rose wondered if she was becoming selfish. By the time she pulled into her drive she realised she was being melodramatic, that what had happened at the mine shaft had left her edgy and more than a little suspicious. On the other hand Nick had offered no more than friendship and if it was Jenny he wanted they could still remain friends. Rose had done nothing to jeopardise his relationship with the younger woman.

Both Laura and Barry had been delighted that she was finally doing what she had been born to do. She was not deserting them, she was simply picking up a career where she had left it off.

Turning her key in the lock she decided she was glad to be home.

# CHAPTER THREE

Jenny Manders was one of the last to leave the gallery. She was quietly seething. How dare Nick be so obvious about Rose in front of her and the people who had known them as a couple. Maddy hadn't wasted any time before making one of her bitchy comments. And what did Rose Trevelyan have that she didn't? She could paint, that was all. I may only be a model, Jenny thought, but I'm fifteen years her junior and better looking. But despite an excess of wine which had made her bitter, she acknowledged the unfairness of her thoughts. Rose was a nice woman. Even Alec Manders, her father, known for his taciturnity and meanness of manner, had seemed drawn to her on the one occasion all three had met in the street. And who the hell does Maddy think she is to be so judgemental when all she produces is tat for the tourists, and she has the gall to imagine she's one of us.

Jenny's pride in her roots was genuine. Unlike many of her contemporaries she had tried life in London and had also spent two months in Paris, mixing with artists on the

53

Left Bank and posing for them. Something in her cried out to be accepted by such people. Although she recognised that she had no talent herself, she fed on those who did. Disappointment had followed disappointment. The Frenchman with whom she had lived for seven of those eight weeks had thrown her out as soon as he was satisfied with the work he had produced using Jenny as his model. Good work, too, for which she would get none of the credit. She had sat shivering for hours in the daytime and shared his bed at night, and all for nothing. With Nick, because it was the longest relationship she had sustained, she had believed it would be different, that he would eventually marry her or at least keep her as his mistress. She would have had the best of all worlds; being amongst the people she admired and both working for and living with an artist, one who could provide a proper home for her.

Her mother had disappeared when she was three years old but she did not learn of the circumstances until she was seventeen. Renata Trevaskis was a beauty, descended from true Romany stock. She had married Alec Manders on her eighteenth birthday but soon became restless and dissatisfied with married life and a small child whose upbringing was mostly taken over by her mother-in-law with whom they had had to live. She started drinking, encouraged by Alec's mother who had never liked her. A year later rumour had it that she had run off with another man, a holidaymaker from somewhere up country. It had surprised no one, knowing the awful restrictions she had had to live under in the strict Chapel environment of the Manders' home.

Agnes Manders was a martinet and had brought her son

up to attend two church services every Sunday. He had, over the years, acquired his mother's views and opinions on everything. Oddly, considering that he believed that women should obey their menfolk, he had always been dominated by his mother. She was the strong one, the one who put food in their mouths and clothed them after his father had died in a mining accident. Because she told him so often, he had grown to believe that she was almost a saint.

Jenny, too, had been brought up on discourses of her grandmother's virtues along with constant reminders of how much she resembled her own mother and that, therefore, she had bad blood in her.

'Why did you marry her, then?' she had asked her father defiantly when she was told her mother's history. The reply had come in the form of a stinging blow across her cheek. Her grandmother, who had been in the room, had hands like steel hawsers.

Once Renata had gone, Jenny's father and his mother tried to curb her natural exuberance but no punishment worked for long. Apart from the time she spent in school she mostly roamed the streets, avoiding the house whenever possible. She suspected it was a relief to both of them when she went away.

As she strolled up the hill, moonlight shining on the cobbles, Jenny pictured her father. He was a squat but well-muscled man, handsome in a lived-in sort of way. A bit like Charles Bronson, Jenny thought, having recently seen a video of one of his films at Stella's. It was easy to see why Angela Choake, a divorcee, had been attracted to him. As soon as Alec's mother had been buried she had moved into the house as her father's wife. Jenny was still in Paris at the time. She had not returned for the funeral, neither had she grieved. She had not loved her grandmother and knew that her own existence had been a thorn in the old woman's side.

Jenny had tired of the sanctimonious ramblings knowing that, for a very long time, it had been her father who was the real provider. He had turned his hand to anything; fishing, mining and back to fishing until he had finally established himself as a reliable jobbing builder.

It was not until a fortnight after her return to St Ives that Jenny learnt that her father had been seeing Angela Choake for many years, but until the demise of her grandmother they had not been out together in public. This led Jenny to understand the power the old woman had had over her son. She had alienated him against his wife and his own daughter. Angela, she thought, was all right. She could have done far worse for a stepmother. Naturally her father had legalised the relationship before allowing Angela to move into the house.

Jenny's return to Cornwall had not been a success. She had moved in with a friend and her husband but, uncomfortable in the midst of their obvious happiness, she left after a month, taking work wherever she could find it and sleeping wherever there was an available bed, occupied already or not.

Then she met Nick and life took an upward turn. That, too, had ended in disaster. She was penniless once more but too proud to let on that she was sleeping in a squat with three other homeless people whom she barely knew.

Jenny did not blame anyone else for her position, nor did she blame herself. She put it down to fate. If she could just get some work things might be better. Work – or a man who was prepared to keep her, that would be even more favourable. All she required was a bit of comfort. But maybe it wasn't too late with Nick. He had not ignored her tonight and was usually friendly if they met by chance and he had gone out of his way to ask how she was. After Rose Trevelyan had left, it was true, but perhaps that meant more than if he had done so whilst she was present. Failing Nick she would fall back on her original plan.

Jenny had drunk all that was offered and had filled up on the food, which solved the problem of that evening's meal. Leaving the gallery she had decided to go and see Nick, a decision she would not have taken with less alcohol inside her.

In the shadows of the old, cramped buildings she felt buoyant. Not one, but two choices, she thought, and clutched her woollen charity shop coat closer to her as she made her way through the deserted streets. Her long skirt flapped around her ankles as the wind funnelled down the narrow alleys she had to negotiate to reach Nick's house. The night held no fears for her; not once had she felt afraid in the place of her birth. It wasn't late, a little after nine-thirty, but she had passed the area where there were pubs and restaurants. Now there were only quiet lanes, each one becoming narrower and narrower and progressively steeper and darker.

Behind the tiny paned windows of the cottages the occasional light showed through thin curtains or those not tightly pulled together. She shivered, pleased to see Nick's porch light shining in welcome. From inside she heard his voice and stood, undecided, before knocking. No other voice replied so she assumed he must be on the telephone, which was near the front door. She lifted the metal ring and let it drop. The dull thud reverberated through the street. Nick let her in, smiling and nodding his intention that she should sit down. He closed the door behind her whilst cradling the telephone receiver between ear and shoulder. 'Okay, I'll see you then. Bye,' he said, giving Jenny no clue as to whom he had been speaking.

'Jenny? What brings you here?'

She would not beg but she wanted to make her position clear. 'I was lonely. I wanted to talk to someone. Well, you, really.'

'Drink?' Nick turned his back and opened the door of an old-fashioned sideboard from which he produced a cheap bottle of brandy. 'Of course we can talk, there was no need for us to fall out at all.'

Jenny thought this was a good start. She took the brandy glass and sat down on the sagging sofa which he had still not got around to replacing and on which they had made love many times. The thought made her maudlin. 'I miss you, Nick,' she said, already aware that she *would* beg if absolutely necessary. 'What went wrong?' She bowed her head submissively. 'Please tell me.'

Nick frowned. If he told her, she would become even more insecure than before; if he didn't, she would think he wanted her back. 'Nothing really went wrong, we just weren't suited.'

'How can you say that?' Her voice was raised. 'We were everything to each other.'

'Jenny, listen. This might come out all wrong, but if I was everything to you, you had a strange way of showing it.'

'What do you mean?'

Nick swirled the brandy in his glass and kept his eyes averted. 'I kept you, Jenny, and I didn't resent that one bit. I was fully aware of your financial position. However, despite my earning both our keep, it was still me who looked after this place and cooked most of our meals.'

'Oh, Nick, I'll cook for you. I'm quite a good cook, you know. And I'll do the cleaning.'

He was embarrassed, not for himself, but for this proud girl who was metaphorically on her knees before him. There was no option but to be cruel. 'It wasn't just that. You never forgave me for going to London alone. That was business, I couldn't have spared the time to entertain you as well. For months after I returned you accused me of all sorts of things. I, apparently, was allowed no freedom, whereas you had as much as if we weren't together at all. Jenny, you, of all people, know how everyone gossips. There were other men during the time you were with me. That bloke who came down from Cheshire, the one you claimed you were posing for—'

'I did pose for him.'

'Accepted, but that's not all you did. He made it pretty obvious in the pubs he drank in. No, Jenny, I'm more than happy to remain your friend and I'll do anything I can to help you, but that's as far as it goes.'

'Because of Rose Trevelyan.'

'No.' He paused. It was true, but since they'd split up he'd used Jenny. He now saw how stupid he had been.

'I suppose she cooks you meals before she lets you screw her.'

Nick stood and walked over to where she was sitting. For a split second Jenny thought he was going to hit her. She flinched but she knew that Nick would never hurt her. He took her by the elbow and lifted her to her feet. 'You're going home now, Jenny. You've had far too much of Stella's excellent wine. Let's both forget this ever happened.'

'I won't forget!' she shouted from outside the closed door. 'I won't forget,' she repeated in time to her hurried, stumbling footsteps as the tears ran down her face.

Ten minutes after she left the telephone rang. It was Maddy. 'Nick, have you seen Jenny since the opening?'

'Yes. She just left here.'

'Ah, I thought so. I was upstairs looking out of the window and I saw her go by coming from your direction. She looked pretty wild, if you ask me. Is she okay?'

'Yes, I think so. She's much tougher than she lets people believe.'

'I just thought I'd check. Hey, why don't you come over tomorrow? I've got four mackerel here which I've cleaned, seems a shame to freeze them. Any time after seven would suit me.'

'I'm not sure, Maddy. Can I let you know in the morning?'

'Of course. No problem.'

Nick hung up. Life was strange. He had been speaking to Rose when Jenny arrived, although she hadn't sounded all that thrilled to hear his voice. The brief conversation had ended by Rose telling him that she was busy until the following weekend. Now Jenny wanted to come back into his life and Maddy, out of the blue, had invited him around for dinner. 'All or nothing,' he muttered, recalling the many months of his life when there had been nobody.

Rose had intended to telephone Barry Rowe upon her return from the gallery but after Nick's call, which had unsettled her for some reason, she had decided to leave it until the morning.

'Rosie! I was beginning to wonder what had happened to you. You're almost a stranger these days.'

She pictured his lean, stoop-shouldered frame, a bony hand pushing his heavily framed glasses up his nose as he answered the phone in the shabbiness of his small flat. He claimed to like where he lived although he could easily have afforded somewhere far nicer. Was he dressed yet or was he wearing the rough woollen dressing gown with its silky girdle that she had seen hanging on the back of the bathroom door? 'I wondered if you'd heard about . . . ?'

'Your most recent escapade? Of course I have, you know how fast news travels here. At least it didn't come to anything. Wait a minute, that's not why you're phoning, is it? Don't tell me that you, in your indomitable way, think there's more to it?'

'No. I made a mistake.'

'Jesus! Did I hear right? Is this the Rose Trevelyan I've known and, well, known for many years? An admission of error, no less.'

Rose smiled. He may have stopped in time but she knew what he had almost said. But had she made a mistake? Logic told her yes but her instincts said no. 'I'm trying to forget it. Anyway, the reason I'm ringing is to invite you for dinner tonight.'

'I'll be there. Seven-thirty okay? I've got to go to the Camborne factory at five.'

'Fine. See you later.'

The forecast had proved to be correct. The sun was rising in a cloudless sky, the air was fresh and clear with a hint of an offshore breeze. Rose went out to the car. It was still a pleasant surprise to turn the car key in the ignition and hear the engine catch immediately. She hesitated before putting it into reverse gear and backing down the drive. I have to go back, she thought. I have to finish that painting.

She barely noticed the drive or the other traffic but anxiously chewed her lip, wondering if she was a fool for being so nervous or a worse one for returning to the old mine. She parked, aware of the sudden silence as she cut the engine, then headed to where she had sat two days ago. Nothing had changed except that some of the scrub had been flattened where the tyres of the emergency vehicles had crushed it. The bracken was crisp, more russet than brown, but the undergrowth still showed signs of green. Lichen-covered rocks, hidden in summer, began to show through as the plants died down. Rose stared at the old engine house, now in ruins, then across to where the adit of the mine lay. She listened but there was no sound apart from the whisper of the bracken and the sighing of the wind as it swept over the bleak landscape and through the bare, twisted trees which had bent to its will and stood no higher than Rose herself. She shook her head. It had to be a trick of acoustics, she thought as she set up her easel and began to work.

Was it Stella, or had Maddy originally suggested this particular location? she wondered. And did it mean anything?

Mortification washed over her again as she recalled the false alarm she had raised. Uneasily she worked, mixing oils on her palette and lining up the scene using the wooden end of a brush. An hour passed and she became absorbed in what she was doing, fascinated with the ruins as they stood in silent testimony to the proud mining history of Cornwall. A kestrel, which she recognised by its long tail, distracted her for more than ten minutes as it soared then hovered high in the sky, head down in typical manner as it searched for prey. Three times it plummeted but Rose did not think it caught anything. She shook her head. There would be no exhibition like Stella's if she didn't get a move on. Swirling the brush in the colour she had mixed for the brickwork which was in shadow, her arm jerked and paint splashed her jeans. 'Dear God, no.' Her voice was strangled as she jumped to her feet. A scream had pierced the air. She swung around, terrified. Had she been mistaken before, there was no doubt about it now. Her hands shook and her legs felt weak. It was hard to judge where it had come from yet it did not contain the thin quality which open air ought to have given it. And, more to the point, what to do now? Impossible to ring for assistance, the only help she could expect would be in the form of men in white coats come to take her away. Rapidly she packed her things, leaving the wet painting on the easel. Then, sick with fright and aware of the risk, Rose picked her way towards the engine house feeling like an actress in a horror film when the audience will her not to go into the empty building. She stood still, listening. Nothing, not a sound except her thumping heart and ragged breathing.

She looked in every direction but there was no sign of life other than the kestrel, now further away looking for richer pickings.

'I've got to get out of here,' she said. 'I must be going mad.'

Panic overcame her. Staggering and half tripping, she turned and ran, grabbing her equipment and throwing it into the back of the car, remembering just in time the wet canvas which she placed, face up, on the front passenger seat. Her foot slipped off the clutch and she reversed jerkily before starting to make her way home.

Never was she so relieved to see her house looking so normal at the top of her drive. It was a little after two and already the sun was less bright. It would set by four o'clock. Not caring what time it was or what anyone might think, the first thing she did was to pour a gin and tonic. If Jack Pearce walked in and called her an alcoholic she wouldn't care. Gin slopped on to the worktop as the bottle clinked against the glass. Ice slipped on to the floor. Rose left it there and took a large sip before switching on all the lights.

The shaking began to lessen but it was an hour before she felt able to clean her brushes and the palette knife and stand the canvas against the wall in the attic studio out of the way of the central heating. Since she rarely used the room now she had turned off the radiator. Thank goodness for the down-to-earth solidity of Barry Rowe, she thought as she lit one of the five cigarettes she allowed herself each day and sat down at the kitchen table to finish her drink and to plan what to cook him for dinner. Something special, she decided, to make up for her neglect. The crab season was over but she had some which she had frozen earlier in the year. She got it out of the freezer, it wouldn't take long to thaw. White and dark meat. She could mix it with soft cheese and make pate with crudites. This would be followed by lamb kebabs marinated in lemon juice, olive oil, garlic and some of Doreen Clarke's redcurrant jelly. Served with rice and a green salad it would appear to have taken more effort than it really had. Rose knew that concentration on the food was a way of subduing the thoughts that wanted to rise to the surface; if she kept calm a perfectly logical explanation would come to mind.

As she crushed the garlic its pungent aroma overrode the fruity smell of the redcurrant jelly which was melting slowly in a small saucepan. Rose enjoyed cooking and the automatic, familiar gestures as she moved around her kitchen soothed her. Outside the night clouds began to gather and soon it was completely dark. Once the table was laid, the pate in individual dishes in the fridge and the rest of the meal ready to cook, Rose went upstairs to change.

She was sitting quietly listening to some music when Barry arrived, his head jutting forward as if he was unsure of his welcome. Rose kissed his cheek, accepted the bottle of wine he had brought and asked him to open it.

'You look a bit pale, you're not going down with something, are you?'

'No, I don't think so.'

He stood, arms folded, and studied her face. 'Rose, tell me what's happened.' It wasn't a question.

Her head jerked up. Had she spoken her thoughts aloud or was he telepathic?

'You're involved in something, Rose, I know it.'

'No. Not involved. Oh, it's ridiculous.'

'You didn't go out there again?'

'I had to, Barry. The painting's good, I know it is. In fact, I'm certain it's the best I've ever done. I couldn't not finish it because of some wild auditory hallucination.'

Barry shrugged and pulled the cork from the bottle. 'The mind can play strange tricks.'

'Yes. You're right. Perhaps I need a holiday.'

'I could do with one myself.'

Rose turned away to put the skewered lamb and peppers under the grill, unprepared to follow up the obvious hint. 'It won't be long.'

They were halfway through the meal. Rose was struggling to eat as Barry regaled her with stories about his customers and complimented her on the food. He knew something was very wrong and was hurt that she wouldn't confide in him, but to press her would be a waste of breath, she would dig her heels in further. All he could do was to offer assistance if she required it. 'Rose?'

She looked up and tried to smile. He was a decent man, solid and dependable, and she often wished she had been able to offer him more. He could also be irritating, domineering and possessive, she reminded herself as the telephone rang causing her to jump. She went to the sitting room to answer it. It was Nick. Rose shuffled backwards, trailing the lead in one hand, and, with the heel of her shoe, nudged the door closed behind her. This is silly, she thought, there was no reason she shouldn't receive a call from whomsoever she pleased. However, she had to take Barry's feelings into consideration. Nick asked how she was. Rose wondered why he was ringing again. Only last night she had told him that she was busy. Was he the sort of man to pester, not to take no for an answer? If so, there was no future for them. That was not the sort of relationship she wanted. A more sinister thought crossed her mind. He knew she had been going back to the mine that day – had he called to find out her reaction to what he may have known would happen?

'No, I haven't,' she answered, puzzled, when Nick asked if she'd seen Jenny. 'Not since we were at Stella's. Why? What's wrong?'

'Probably nothing. She came to see me afterwards. Rose, I ought to have told you sooner, we were once . . .'

'Yes. I thought so. You don't have to explain, Nick.' And she meant it. At least he was being honest with her.

'Well, good. Anyway, as I was saying, she came up here wanting to make a go of things again. It was all over more than six months ago and there was no chance of my agreeing. In retrospect I see I could've been kinder. She was in a bit of a state when she left. Maddy rang me to say she'd seen her running down the road in tears.'

Rose couldn't see where this was leading.

'I felt bad about it. I mean, I loved the girl once. Did you know she's staying in a squat?'

'No. I didn't.'

'Well, nor did I until today. I went down there. The crowd she shares with haven't seen her since yesterday morning. We know she was all right when she left my place. I'm probably worrying about nothing, Jenny can look after herself. If she was that upset she may not have fancied facing her friends.'

'But why would I have seen her?'

'Oh, God. Look, I just thought, well, she made one or two insinuations about us. She was drunk and upset. I thought she may have come to see you, to persuade you to give me up or to put you off me. Besides, you're out and about a lot, I thought you may simply have run into her somewhere.'

'No, Nick, I'm sorry. The last time I saw her she was still at Stella's.'

'Okay, thanks anyway. I expect she'll turn up when she's got whatever it is out of her system. I hope I'm not interrupting anything?' he asked with a question in his voice.

Rose hesitated. 'I've got a dinner guest.'

'I see.'

No, you don't, she thought, but was not prepared to explain.

'Rose, can I still see you next Saturday? We could make a day of it, go to Truro and shop and have a meal.'

She was surprised that she didn't hesitate in agreeing. 'I shall look forward to it,' she said. And that was as much encouragement as Nick Pascoe was getting. If he was so worried about Jenny, a girl, or woman, with whom he had once been close, one who now chose to live or sleep wherever she pleased, then he must still care for her. It was none of her business. She still loved David and always would. You don't necessarily stop caring for someone just because you're no longer together, she reminded herself.

Putting on a cheerful smile she returned to the kitchen to find Barry cleaning his glasses on the edge of the tablecloth in a manner so nonchalant she guessed he had made a determined effort not to eavesdrop on her side of the conversation. She felt exhausted and was glad when he said he must go because he was seeing another of his artists early in the morning.

As she lay in bed the weather began to echo the turmoil of her thoughts. The breeze, which had sent tremors through the shrubs as Barry was leaving, gained strength and whistled in the chimney breast. The windows rattled as the wind increased to gale force. The house was taking the blasts from the front. Rose was unconcerned about damage. The place had survived numerous storms, worse ones than this, and the roof had been replaced a couple of years ago after slates had been ripped off and flung into the garden.

In the end she had decided against telling Barry what had happened. For once she would have welcomed the listening ear of Jack Pearce and almost found herself missing him. Perhaps, she admitted, that was only because he was a foil for her eccentric friends.

Rose did not believe that Jenny was the sort of girl to do a disappearing act simply to gain the attention of a man, but she didn't know her well enough to be certain. And there was, she decided as she turned over to find a more comfortable position, little enough for Jenny to be jealous of. If anything, it ought to be the reverse. Jenny was young and beautiful with a softness of body and face few possessed.

When she woke the violence of the wind had not abated although it had veered to the west and, with it, brought squally rain. The sky had hardly lightened by the time she had showered and dressed and by nine-thirty it was obvious that the weather was set for the day. The view Rose so loved was obscured. The Mount, shrouded in rain, might not have existed. To cheer the place up she lit the fire, which smoked infuriatingly for half an hour before finally catching properly. There was no reason for her to leave the house. The fridge was well stocked and she could put the final touches to the painting in the attic where she had splashed out on an overhead light fitting which produced the next best thing to daylight.

Against her better judgement Rose still took the odd photographic commission, which Laura had told her was a sop to her insecurity.

'I don't want to lose my touch,' Rose had argued.

'What you mean is you're afraid you'll fail and you'll need something to fall back on.'

Is she right? Rose wondered as she carried a mug of coffee upstairs to develop the one roll of film that was outstanding. Twice she was interrupted, once by Stella who had now heard that Jenny had gone into hiding, although this was not the main reason for the call. She was ringing to ask if Rose would come to a party they were having on 23rd December. 'It's the only effort we make,' Stella added. 'All our friends come in one go. After that we lock ourselves in and ignore Christmas. I suppose if we'd had children it might've been different. Do come.'

'I'd love to. Thanks.' Rose scribbled herself a reminder note then, without time to think about what she was saying, said, 'In which case I hope you'll come to me on New Year's Eve.'

'I'll check with Daniel but I'm sure the answer'll be yes. Goodness, we haven't done that for donkey's years.'

And neither have I, Rose thought, wondering what she had let herself in for. A party? Not since the early years of her marriage had she thrown one. It was an exciting thought.

'Did you do any work on your painting yesterday? I managed to get out for an hour or so and make the most of the weather.'

'Yes.' Rose waited but Stella made no further comment. For the first time she wondered how genuine her friend's interest was.

On her way back upstairs she realised that there wasn't much time. If she was seriously going to throw a party she must organise the invitations quickly before people made other arrangements, if they hadn't done so already.

The second call was from Barry to inform her that they had sold out of the wildflower notelets and he wanted her permission to do a reprint. Rose said yes, knowing that he need not have asked, she always agreed, but that he often found excuses to talk to her. When she mentioned the party,

Barry stuttered his acceptance. He was as amazed as Rose had been at the idea.

Leaving the film to dry prior to making prints, Rose stared at the almost complete oil. It disturbed her because of its associations and if it wasn't so good she might have destroyed it. But it is good, she thought, very good. Ought I to tell someone, even if it does make me look ridiculous? she asked herself as she began mixing colours which would put the final touches to the painting.

It was early evening and she was cleaning her brushes when she thought she heard a noise downstairs. Standing still, she listened. From two flights up she could not always be sure if it was the wind or a knock on the kitchen door. She wiped her paint-stained hands on a rag and went to see. Leaning against the jamb, soaking wet, was Inspector Jack Pearce. Rose bit her lip. What now? Why did he keep having to bother her? Seconds later she saw that he wasn't alone.

'May we come in?'

'Yes.' Rose stood back and held the door open, shutting it quickly as rain gusted in. She switched on the fluorescent light to dispel the gloom, knowing that this was no social visit.

'Just a few questions,' Jack said in a voice more official than she had heard before.

'Please, do sit down.'

Jack pulled out a chair and introduced the younger man as Detective Sergeant Green. It was he who took notes whilst Jack asked the questions. 'Three days ago you rang the emergency services regarding what you thought was a scream coming from near or inside the old mine shaft.'

Rose waited. If this was another game to humiliate her further she would threaten to make an official complaint. She was certainly not about to mention the second occasion.

'What made you think there might be someone there?'

'Look, Jack, I've better things to do with my time than play games with you. I admit, I was wrong. I thought I heard a scream, later it was proved that I couldn't have done.' Sergeant Green's eyebrows shot up at her use of his first name.

Jack did not fail to notice Rose blushing. 'That's not what I meant. Have you any reason to believe anyone uses the place for whatever activities they think fit? You know, drugs, orgies, painting, like yourself? Witchcraft?'

Rose laughed. 'None at all. That place is always deserted.'

'Thank you. Just one more thing. When did you last see Jennifer Manders?'

'Two nights ago. I was at the opening of Stella Jackson's latest exhibition. Jenny was there as well.'

'Not since?'

'No.' So Nick had been more than a little concerned if it had reached the stage of police involvement.

'And you wouldn't have any idea where she might be staying?'

'Jack, I hardly know her. I've met her less than a dozen times, mostly at Stella's, once with her father. We haven't reached the stage of exchanging confidences.'

It was Jack's turn to raise a sardonic eyebrow as if he found this unlikely. His next words confirmed her suspicion.

'I'd say that was unusual, wouldn't you? People do seem to have a tendency to confide in you.'

'I don't know where she is,' Rose replied firmly. 'Nor do I have any idea why she's disappeared.'

It was a mistake. She knew that as soon as she had uttered the words.

'I didn't say she's disappeared.'

'Then why are you asking these questions? Her friends in St Ives will be far more use to you than I could be.' Damn him, she thought, feeling his dark eyes on her face: he probably believed she knew more than she did and was holding something back. The fact that this was true made her uncomfortable.

'If you do hear anything you'll let us know, won't you?' It was an order rather than a polite request.

'Her father,' Rose added, recalling the firm, interesting features of Alec Manders. 'Have you tried him? She might be staying there.'

Jack didn't answer. Instead he stood, nodded to his silent companion and made his way to the door. 'Sorry to have troubled you, Mrs Trevelyan.'

Rose closed the door behind him. The formality hurt and it shouldn't have done. The agreement was that they remained friends but Jack didn't seem to want it that way. She peered into the fridge trying to decide what she fancied to eat. Jenny Manders had only been missing for a few hours short of two days. Rose thought it odd that so much was being made of her disappearance. So soon, anyway. She shrugged. There were probably factors she knew nothing about and there was no way she was going to allow

74

Jack to involve her. 'But I think I'm already involved.' She spoke aloud as a terrible thought crossed her mind. Could it possibly have been Jenny whose screams she had heard? No. Jenny had been at Stella's after that first occasion. She shook her head. The painting was finished, there was no need to go there ever again.

# CHAPTER FOUR

Jack Pearce was thoughtful during the drive back towards Camborne. It had been a deliberate policy to take someone with him because whenever he encountered Rose he was unsure how he would react. Her rejection still hurt. And, he admitted, he had made the visit in an official capacity although someone of lower rank would normally have done so.

Rose was not inclined to panic. After his initial anger he had realised that some good reason must have prompted her to make that call. Now Jennifer Manders was missing – and Rose knew the girl. He was sure there was more to it than a lovers' tiff or whatever they called it these days. Jenny may be hiding out, sulking, or she could have taken off, alone or with another man, but from what they had learnt it was unlikely that she would have left the area.

Madeleine Duke, Stella Jackson, her husband Daniel Wright, and the girl's father and his wife had all been questioned; all had expressed the opinion that she would not have strayed far. If it wasn't for the suspicions that were aroused every time Rose came into the equation he doubted if he would have paid much attention to Nick Pascoe's telephone call despite the fact that the man had sounded genuinely worried.

The three with whom she shared the squat had been unhelpful. They resented the police and, not knowing Jenny well, neither knew nor cared what might have become of her. All they were prepared to say was that they hadn't seen her for a couple of days. It might be worth paying Pascoe a personal visit, he thought. 'Take the St Ives turn-off,' he told DS Green who was driving.

According to Pascoe, Jennifer Manders had been after a reconciliation but he wasn't having it and had sent her away. But had he sent her somewhere permanently? Now who's being fanciful? he asked himself. Had he done so, Pascoe would hardly have drawn attention to the fact.

Nick was upstairs in the room he used to store his work, sorting through frames for a forthcoming show in which he was to be one of half a dozen exhibitors. He was still deciding on the last two of the ten canvases he was expected to display when he heard the crash of the knocker.

'You'd better come in,' he said, frowning, when he learnt who his visitor was. DS Green had been asked to wait in the car.

Jack wiped his feet on the coarse doormat and stepped straight into the living area of the low-ceilinged dwelling. Its small windows and the proximity of other similar properties rendered it dark even on a sunny day. Now, on a wet winter's evening, it was positively gloomy despite the two table lamps. The room was chilly but not damp. Pascoe was a hardy man; the sash window was open six inches. Ahead was a wooden staircase, beside it an open door leading to the kitchen. To Jack's right was the back of the settee with its sagging springs and against the wall by the window stood a table and four chairs. On it were the remains of a single meal. There were no shelves. Pascoe's books and cassettes were stacked on the floor beside the player. Neither was there a television set, possibly because there was no room for one, or maybe it was kept in the bedroom.

Jack had surveyed the room in seconds, and now turned his attention to the man. His mouth tightened. He could understand why Rose was attracted to him. Not only was he an artist but he possessed rugged good looks and he had a way of moving which suggested that he was totally comfortable in the world.

Standing with his hands in the pockets of his denim jacket, Nick asked if there was any news.

'No. None.' Fighting for objectivity in the face of the man who had replaced him, Jack asked him to go over the night in question again. It would be all too easy to apportion blame here and thus effectively remove the opposition. But blame for what?

'Certainly.' Nick hooked out a chair with the toe of his suede boot and sat down. Jack chose the settee when it was indicated that he should do the same, then regretted it as he sank low into the cushions. 'Jenny turned up at Stella's exhibition. She was there before me. I wasn't certain if I could attend.'

'She was invited?'

'Jenny? Yes, definitely. She was there for the drinks upstairs before the official opening. I didn't see much of her in the gallery, there were too many other people there, but we managed a few words. I left before she did and came straight home. About forty-five minutes later, possibly more, she knocked on the door and I let her in. I was on the phone at the time to Rose Trevelyan.'

Jack flinched. He could have hit the man but he listened carefully as Pascoe went over the events of that evening.

'That's it. It's exactly as I said before on the phone. Oh, then Maddy rang. Madeleine Duke.'

'For any specific reason?'

'Out of concern for Jenny. She knows Jenny can be a bit highly strung, if that phrase is still in fashion. She also wanted to invite me to supper the next night.'

Jack nodded. The man was certainly in demand and he wondered if Rose knew. But he would not lower himself to ask if he had accepted the invitation. 'And yesterday morning?'

'Yesterday morning I began to worry about what Maddy had said. Jenny's impetuous, the sort of girl who is capable of doing something stupid to draw attention to herself, but I didn't know where she was staying. I asked around and when her three – what shall we say, room-mates? – said they hadn't seen her either I decided I ought to call the police.'

'You went out of your way to find her?'

'Naturally. I wouldn't waste your time if I thought I could locate her myself.' Nick had felt the right thing to do was to report Jenny missing but he had not expected any action to be taken. Now he asked himself why an inspector was involved. It worried him.

'And who did you ask?'

'Everyone who was at the exhibition. The people I know, that is.'

'Including Mrs Trevelyan?' He couldn't help it even though he knew the answer.

'Yes.'

'Why?'

Nick's frown deepened but did not detract from his good looks. 'Just in case she'd seen Jenny.'

'Mrs Trevelyan lives in Newlyn. What made you think she might have done?'

'Nothing made me think so, Inspector. It was just that she was there and, well, Jenny knew that we'd been seeing each other.'

'But your affair with Jennifer Manders was over. Why should it concern her who you're seeing now?'

'Look, I don't really know. I've already explained she wanted to come back here to live. If she was jealous, I thought she might have gone to Rose's to cause a scene. Really, I'm not a mind reader, it was only a guess.'

He has a temper, Jack thought, as Nick got up and strode around the room, sweeping back his hair impatiently as he did so. And what had caused Pascoe to think Jenny had been to see Rose? He sighed, knowing there was little more he could do. But as he stood he thought it worth a try to ask, 'Did Mrs Trevelyan tell you she called us recently? She—'

'When she was out at the old engine house? Yes.'

'Was anyone aware she'd be there that day?'

'How on earth should I know?' Nick stopped pacing. He picked up a paintbrush and slapped the bristles against the palm of his hand. 'Actually, now I think about it, quite a lot of people. It was Stella who suggested it as a starting place. There was a crowd of us there one night when the subject came up.'

'By which you mean?'

'Rose has gone back to working in oils, and not before time if what I've seen of her work's anything to go by. Stella thought it'd be a test for her. So many artists have painted just that type of scenery but if Rose could do it, and do it well, or better, it would prove that she wasn't run-of-the-mill. Stella thought it would give her the confidence to carry on.'

'I'll need the names of the guests that night, if you don't mind.'

Nick provided them and Jack left, more puzzled than when he had arrived. Had those screams had anything to do with Jenny's disappearance even if she had been seen afterwards? There was one way of settling something which bothered him and he believed he could arrange it with very little outlay. He was owed a favour from several years back. One he decided it was time to call in. This was unofficial business. If nothing came of it he would not, like Rose, have made a public fool of himself.

Madeleine Duke's past life was mostly unknown to her Cornish friends and this was part of the reason why she hadn't been accepted with as much enthusiasm as she had expected. True, invitations came at regular intervals, such as the one to Stella's exhibition, and there was never a shortage of visitors to her shop or the flat above it, but she still felt she was treated differently. Already she was beginning to realise that her past, good or bad, didn't matter here. What did matter was that she refused to talk about it. What she had failed to understand was that she would have been welcomed more warmly if the details of her life were common knowledge. The Cornish possessed a need to know but for no reason other than to satisfy their innate curiosity. Nothing would have been held against her.

Maddy had had a child, a daughter, and for this sin, because she had been unmarried, her parents had disowned her. She had realised too late that she was pregnant, and a termination was out of the question. The baby had been adopted. It was some years ago now but she still regretted it and the pain remained. How happy the child would have been in Cornwall if only she'd been allowed a chance to think things through. But it was too late now. An only child herself, she had been the centre of her parents' world, only to be told how cruelly she had let them down in the end. Having Annie, as she secretly called the little girl, adopted had not healed the breach between them as she had believed it would. Her parents had refused to have anything more to do with her. Maddy had given away her child for nothing. She had moved down to Brighton and mixed with a crowd her parents would have loathed until it dawned on her that they were losers like herself. From there she had moved from town to town along the south coast, never finding the sense of belonging that she was searching for. Finally she had come to Cornwall where, after two years of constant grind, cleaning and serving in cafes and pubs, she had saved enough to add to the small sum her grandmother, who had secretly sympathised with her, had left her and rented the tiny shop and the premises above it. In the little spare time she had had Maddy had worked at her crafts and, although initially her stock was sparse, she had continued to add to it, buying in when necessary.

Just over a year ago, after a particularly successful summer, she had spoken to her landlord and made him an offer to buy which had been accepted. Now she had a mortgage hanging over her head but instead of worrying her it gave her the sense of security which she had been lacking since the adoption of her baby when her life had been turned upside down. She lived frugally but was almost content. Only one thing really mattered: tracing her daughter. But that was not her prerogative, legally it must be the other way around. Maddy realised she was nest-building in case of that happy eventuality.

Her need to belong was so desperate that even she realised it was unnatural. Other women, women like Rose Trevelyan, seemed quite content to go it alone and regarded being accepted as neither here nor there. Perhaps that was the secret, not to care too much. Rose Trevelyan was an outsider, too, although she had married a Cornishman and had lived in the area for over twenty-five years.

She had been rearranging the stock on the shelves during a quiet period when a policeman had arrived to question her about Jenny Manders. Maddy had been unusually withdrawn and barely spoke other than to confirm that she had seen Jenny when she went past in tears but had no idea where she might have gone. 'If she was that upset she could've come here, she'd have seen the light on,' she had added. 'She knows me well enough for that.' A customer looking for Christmas presents had come in and the policeman had gone.

Later that afternoon Stella, who had closed the gallery early, dropped in for a chat. There was still no news of Jenny. Maddy Duke did not know how she was supposed to react but she managed to keep her feelings hidden. She was still smarting. from the disappointment at Nick's refusal to share her mackerel.

The following morning, after a fitful sleep, Maddy stood behind the glass of the shop door and watched the teeming rain. Water ran over the cobbles and down towards the harbour. Some of the galleries were open. Last-minute Christmas shoppers huddled beneath umbrellas and stepped back, pressing against the buildings to avoid being splashed, when a car passed through the narrow lanes. She sighed. What's done is done, she thought. It's too late to change things now. She had not lied to the police, except by omission. Wanting Nick, she hoped he would show his gratitude in the way in which she desired once he learnt how she had protected him from what might have been a potentially awkward situation.

Rose stared out of the window. It was Sunday evening. 'It's still raining,' she commented unnecessarily.

'It was forecast,' Laura said, getting up stiffly from the

85

floor with a groan. 'It'll probably last through Christmas now.'

The two women looked at each other and smiled. Long wet spells were very much a part of their lives and the conversations that were conducted in the local shops. The sharp, cold weather, if it came at all, never lasted and Christmas Day was almost always mild, if not warm.

They had been sharing a bottle of wine in Rose's sitting room and talking about the Newlyn lights which had recently been switched on. Then, on the night of 19th December, they would go off in memory of the crew of the lifeboat *Solomon Browne* who, in 1981, lost their lives in a desperate bid to save those of others.

The switching on of the lights was an event and crowds came to witness it, along with the fireworks, and to listen to the male voice choir, although it was to Mousehole the coach parties went to see the displays, some of which floated in the harbour or were fixed high up on the hills.

Unlike most places, Newlyn and Mousehole preferred to wait; their lights were lit mid-December during the Christmas season proper, not two months in advance.

'I haven't heard one word about Nick Pascoe this evening,' Laura commented slyly as she refilled their glasses.

Rose, curled in an armchair, shrugged.

'Are you going to see him again?' Laura rewound the band restraining her hair before resuming her position, cross-legged on the floor in front of the fire. She had taken off her boots because the toes were damp and, despite the horizontal stripes of her Lycra leggings, her legs still looked thin. Rose couldn't remember the last time she'd seen her friend in a skirt.

'Yes. On Saturday.'

'You don't sound over-enthusiastic.'

'I'm not.'

'Come on, Rose. Tell Auntie Laura.'

'Oh, I don't know. I just don't want to rush into things.'

'Dear God, woman, you waited five years to get involved with another man, I wouldn't call that rushing. Okay, I accept that you and Jack wasn't to be, but Nick's an artist and you've got lots in com—Oh, Rose. Don't!' Laura was on her feet, pulling a tissue from the sleeve of her thigh-length tabard. 'What have I said? Me and my big mouth.'

Rose wiped her eyes and sniffed. 'It's not you, Laura. It's me. I don't know what I want any more. I don't even know if I want anyone else. I enjoy male company but it was David I loved. You see, I was lucky, I had the best. I don't see why there needs to be anyone else.'

'There doesn't,' Laura said decisively, perching on the arm of Rose's chair. 'No one can replace David but you mustn't close your mind to the possibility that there could be someone else out there who would be equally right. Different, yes, but still right.' Laura pursed her lips and stared over Rose's head. 'I think you're talking to the wall, Laura Penfold.'

Rose managed a smile. 'I'll bear in mind what you said. It's just that I thought I was finally over it. It's a long time since I cried.'

Laura hugged her. 'No harm in that. And you'll cry

again. There'll always be times when you feel like this, but you still have to live, my girl.' She took Rose's glass. 'Come on, we'll never get drunk at this rate. Now, what else is bothering you?'

'Honestly! Can't I have any secrets?'

'You should know better than that when I'm around.'

'You've got to tell Jack,' Laura said when Rose had told her what had happened on her return visit to the mine. 'Especially if this girl has gone missing. There might be a connection.'

Rose knew she was right, but now she would have to endure his wrath for *not* reporting it. 'Okay, I'll do it.'

Laura said she was going home because there was something she wanted to watch on television. After she left, Rose debated whether to have a bath and an early night with a book or to watch the programme herself. She did neither because Jack turned up ten minutes later. She swallowed hard. She had not kept her promise to Laura to ring him immediately. Still, she could rectify that now in person.

'Rose, I need to talk to you. Nothing personal,' he added quickly, seeing the sceptical look on her face. 'May I come in?' She looks pale, he thought, and troubled, but still lovely despite that baggy old jumper.

'I'm very tired, Jack, as long as you're quick.'

Jack sighed and sat down, uninvited. 'We've found the remains of a female.' He paused, wondering what the rest of the news would do to Rose. She was frowning. 'In the shaft.'

'What?' Rose's hand flew to her mouth as she sagged into a chair. 'Is it Jenny?'

'Not a body, Rose, remains.'

Her eyes widened with realisation. 'You mean bones? A skeleton?' Jack nodded.

'Well, obviously it's not Jenny then. She's only been missing for three days. And it can't have anything to do with the other screams I heard.'

'What other screams?' Jack leant forward, glaring at her.

'I think I'd better explain, Jack.'

'I think you better had, Rose.'

She did so, aware of his anger and knowing how impossible what she was telling him sounded.

'How the devil do you always get into these situations?' he said, but it was a rhetorical question.

Rose squeezed her forehead between her outspread fingers. 'Wait a minute. The rescue team checked the mine. How come they didn't find anything?'

'They looked at the bottom of the shaft, not further in along it.'

Rose did not seem to be listening. 'Found? What do you mean found? Did someone just decide to pop down there for a quick look?'

'No. I got a rock-climbing friend of mine to do me a favour. Look, don't take this amiss. I know you, Rose, you're not inclined to dramatise and it seems now that there *was* something going on out there. What you heard may have been genuine or some sort of attempt to scare you off. However, what we need to do now is to identify the woman.'

Rose was genuinely tired and emotionally exhausted and none of what she was hearing made sense. She wished

Jack could explain it all away and she could forget about it. 'Will you be able to?'

'We don't know yet. It's been a long time. We'll have to go back over missing persons and hope the pathologists can give us something to work on. I just thought I'd let you know. I wanted to tell you myself rather than you hear it through the grapevine.' He was worried about Rose on two counts. Firstly because he did not believe she had imagined she'd heard something. Although nothing or no one had been found, Rose was too level-headed to have panicked for no reason. And, secondly, if the long-dead woman turned out to have been murdered there was a chance that Rose might be in danger for having drawn attention to the place.

He was suddenly aware that she had been crying before his arrival. She certainly looked as if she had had enough for one day. He got up to leave. Glancing back over his shoulder as he opened the back door, he saw Rose sitting motionless at the table, her head in her hands. Leave it, Jack, he thought, wanting nothing more than to comfort her. 'Goodnight, Rose.'

'Goodnight.' She barely raised her head.

Rose sighed deeply. She was tired and knew that she ought to eat but could not face doing so. Instead she locked up and switched off the lights and went upstairs to get ready for bed. Lying beneath the covers she tried to think of anything other than the body of a stranger lying forgotten at the bottom of the shaft. Cornwall was full of superstition and there were stone circles and ancient places of worship where people claimed to feel power if they touched the stones. This had not happened to Rose but she did wonder if she had experienced some sort of supernatural episode.

The sound of gulls woke her. Above the rattle of rain on the window she heard their noisy squawking as they fought over scraps. Rose drew back the curtains and confronted the gloom of another wet morning. She showered quickly and dressed before making coffee. She intended to buy Barry's present and organise her New Year's Eve party, although at the moment it was the last thing she felt like doing. It puzzled her that Jack had said little regarding her having heard a second scream but she doubted he would leave it at that.

The wipers flicked effectively back and forth across the windscreen as she drove along the sea front. It was mild and muggy, the sort of atmosphere in which germs bred easily and would bring about the misery of colds and flu. The windows steamed up. She started winding down the one beside her before remembering that the demister in this car worked.

Christmas trees twinkled in windows as she made her way towards the Jubilee Pool and Ross Bridge which spanned Penzance harbour. *Scillonian III*, the ferry which made daily trips over to St Mary's, was now laid up for the winter. Rose pulled into the large car-park which had once been part of the harbour before it was filled in and where a space was always guaranteed.

The drizzle was gentle on her face and misted her hair as she walked up Market Jew Street. At the top she turned down into Chapel Street and was cheered by a lively conversation with Tim and Katherine who ran the bookshop where she called to collect the two hardback novels she had ordered as her Christmas present to herself. There was still the question of what to get for Barry but that would have to wait. Although the rain had stopped Rose no longer felt like shopping and she had a sudden desire to be on her own.

At home, coffee beside her and pen and paper at hand, she made a list of friends and acquaintances. Planning the food and drink for the party would provide a welcome distraction from her muddled thoughts. She chewed the mangled cap of the biro. Barry Rowe had already accepted, as had Laura and Trevor. Stella had not yet come back to her so she made a note to ring her and Daniel again. There was Mike and Barbara, Maddy Duke and Nick. And Jenny? Well that would depend upon whether she turned up by then. Nine people, apart from Jenny, ten with herself. It was not many. On the other hand, had she been asked to draw up a list of her friends a year ago there would have been even fewer names. Jack? She shook her head, unsure how he would react to such an invitation. A fleeting smile crossed her face. How about Doreen and Cyril Clarke? They were nice people. Doreen was the same age as Rose but dressed and acted as though she might be her mother. Cyril was an ex-miner who now threw all his energies into his garden. She added their names. I will ask Jack, she decided. I want him to be my friend. Thirteen people. It couldn't be helped, and not everyone might be available.

Half an hour later she had completed a suitable menu. All she had to do now was to plan the location of her next piece of work. St Michael's Mount had been photographed and painted from every conceivable angle and in every type of light and weather.

Rose did not think the market could bear another canvas of that famous view. Besides, it was time to experiment. She preferred rugged scenery or rough seas but she wanted to attempt something more gentle, a country setting, where there were trees and maybe running water, the type of thing she had always been able to capture in watercolours but had not attempted in oils.

Taking the guest list to the sitting room she received affirmative replies from everyone, along with gossip and speculation over the finding of the unknown female. With the exception of Jack, whom she was nervous of asking, Maddy was last on the list. She asked if she might bring a guest.

'Peter Dawson,' she explained. 'Do you know him?'

'Only by reputation. I'd love to meet him.'

As soon as she replaced the receiver, the telephone rang. 'Who on earth have you been talking to? I thought I'd never get through. Rose, can I ask you a favour? Terry and Marie have decided to stay on until after the New Year. Any chance of them coming on the 31st?'

'Of course. I'd love to see them.' Any of Laura's sons was guaranteed to liven up a party should it show signs of flagging. If Jack accepted, that would take the number to sixteen, enough to fill the small house and create a proper party atmosphere. Rose shivered. It was not Jack who made her nervous but his alter ego, Inspector Pearce, who had eventually believed her when she said she had heard screams and who had, because of this, discovered a dead woman. And somehow she was involved, or would become involved – she knew that instinctively. 'Laura, they've found someone in that shaft. Whoever it is, she's been there for years. Jack told me last night.'

'That's a bit too much of a coincidence, isn't it? And how come they didn't find her before?'

Rose explained as much as she knew. 'Look, why don't we meet for a drink tonight if you're not doing anything?'

'Okay. Sevenish in the Swordfish?'

Rose hung up. Arms folded, she wandered across to the window. A widening band of blue was gradually pushing upward from the horizon. Above, clouds parted and spokes of sunlight fanned down to the sea. How odd, she thought, watching the changing vista, a girl goes missing but another female body turns up. But there was work to be done. Upstairs that roll of developed film was waiting to be printed. She decided to get that task out of the way.

Later, having typed out the invoice and boxed up the prints, Rose left them on the hall table to remind herself to deliver them. It was too early to meet Laura so she switched on the television to watch *Westcountry Live,* the hour-long regional news programme. Half seated, she aimed the remote control at the screen and changed channels just in time to hear the newscaster say, 'The body of a woman was discovered this morning near Godrevy Point. She has been identified as Jennifer Manders from St Ives who was recently reported missing. The cause of death is uncertain as the police have not yet issued a statement but they are appealing for the public to come forward with information as to her whereabouts if she has been seen since Thursday night. This is the number to ring.' It appeared at the bottom of the screen. 'We will repeat that number later in the programme. And now we move on to the latest dilemma facing West Country fishermen.'

But Rose was no longer listening. Jenny was dead. It was impossible to accept. The telephone rang. Rose ignored it, the answering machine would pick up the call, she was not ready to speak to anyone yet. Poor Jenny, she thought, so lovely and far too young to have died. Selfishly, Rose felt glad that her body had not been found anywhere near the mine. She would not have been able to cope with that.

Hardly aware that the television was still on, she wondered whether it was suicide or an accident. She might have fallen from the rocks or drowned in the sea. The bulletin had given no clues. The phone rang again. She let it, hearing the machine click into action once more. The sound was down so she had no idea if it was the same caller or a different one.

The small clock on the mantelpiece with its brass base and domed glass cover chimed the hour. Seven o'clock already. She would be late for Laura. Throwing on a raincoat she grabbed her handbag and left the house, slamming the kitchen door behind her.

The street lights were reflected in the water of the harbour and on the glistening pavements which had not yet dried after another brief shower. Three cars came up the hill, thumping music pulsating from one. Another, badly corroded by the salty air, spluttered noisily and belched fumes from a faulty exhaust. The driver of the third tooted but had passed before Rose had a chance to see who it was.

She reached the Strand and hurried to the pub. The Swordfish was unusual in that it had retained two bars. The smaller lounge was carpeted and cosy and might almost have been someone's front room. The long public bar was far more basic with its wooden floor and jukebox. Laura was perched on a high stool talking to two of Trevor's friends. Rose knew them by sight and smiled. They moved away after saying hello.

'The usual?' Laura asked, getting out her purse. She ordered a glass of wine and paid for it then looked Rose full in the face. 'What is it? Are you still upset about last night?'

'No.' Rose turned and dragged a spare stool hearer to Laura. Both women were in jeans and sweatshirts, their hair feathery from the damp atmosphere. 'They've found Jenny.'

'Oh, that's good.' She paused and met Rose's eyes. 'Jesus, not good, I take it.'

'No. She's dead. It was on the news this evening.'

Laura shook her head and her hair, held high on her head in a band, danced wildly. 'What happened?'

'They didn't say, only that her body had been found.'

'Has Jack said anything about it?'

'No.' Rose wondered if it had been him on the telephone rather than one of the St Ives crowd.

They sipped in silence for a while, oblivious to the rock music blaring out and the crashing of the table-football game in progress. 'Laura, I think I'll go home if you don't mind.'

'Of course not. You shouldn't have come, you could have rung me.'

They parted company in the street and went their separate ways. Rose had a lot to think about. Why, for instance, had Jack made such a point of searching the shaft and who was the woman they had found? What relevance, if any, did their findings have to Jenny's death?

But most puzzling of all were those screams. Why would anyone wish to draw attention to the place even if they hadn't known what lay beneath the ground?

# CHAPTER FIVE

Maddy Duke had rung Peter Dawson to ask him to accompany her to Rose's party. He had agreed to do so. When she rang a second time to invite him to her own party, arranged on the spur of the moment for Boxing Day, he had been surprised to hear himself accept another invitation because he was not gregarious.

He was considered to be eccentric, even by Cornish standards. Yet as an artist he was far from flamboyant; he cared little whether his work sold or not because his love was the act of painting, not the income received from it. He lived alone in a two-bedroomed house perched high overlooking the sea between St Ives and Zennor. His abstracts sold for a lot of money, maybe only one or two a year but he knew the danger of flooding the market. Many of his pieces were kept from the public eye until he believed it was time to produce another. He had investments which provided an adequate income for his basic lifestyle and he preferred to live where he did rather than in a better property which would be too big for a single person. He had no intention of sharing his home with anyone and, although many might not agree, it was comfortable enough for him. Now and then he needed a woman but usually went out of the area to find one because the local available females knew better than to expect more than one night in his bed. If he succeeded in seducing Maddy Duke he knew that she was unlikely to prove to be the exception. However, there was something about her which appealed to his baser instincts. She struck him as a passionate woman, one who, involved in her own business, would not make demands on him or expect more than he had to offer. This, he supposed, had been at the back of his mind when he had accepted the invitations. Dress was informal, she had told him, but then it usually was. Peter only bothered with a suit on his rare trips to London.

His house was built of granite and was simply furnished but was not without its touches of luxury. A modern heating system ensured that it was always warm in winter and that there was a constant supply of hot water. He ate well and the cigars he smoked were bought from a specialist shop in Truro. His single malt whisky was delivered by the case from an off-licence in Penzance. With an occasional woman thrown in, Peter Dawson could not imagine what else any man could possibly wish for.

He stood gazing critically at his latest, as yet incomplete, work which was propped on a chair. Whatever the cynics may think, the shapes and colours displayed on the canvas made perfect sense to him. His head on one side, his chin in his hand, he decided that there was a definite pattern in what seemed like randomness.

He moved languidly across the room, cigar smoke trailing behind him and masking the smell of oil paint and turpentine. From his window he saw the lights of a fishing-boat as it returned to the harbour and a scattering of stars which promised a cold night. He would be warm, not so Jenny Manders who would now be in the mortuary in her refrigerated container. He had heard the news on Radio Cornwall as he pottered around in the kitchen making a list for his next visit to the shops.

Jenny had spent the occasional night in his bed and he had fond memories of her. She had been undemanding, accepting that all that was in it for her was the chance to share a few drinks, a simple meal and his body. The arrangement had suited them both and neither of them was offended when they spoke of other lovers. In fact, he thought with a grin, between us we knew enough to make a lot of people sweat.

He sighed and ran a hand through his short hair. It was greying now, but not noticeably so because it was fair and had once been the colour of ripening wheat. Poor cow, he thought, knowing that in reality Jenny had only ever loved Nick. But I understood her, he realised. Loving Nick had not stopped her from sleeping with other men, but her conquests had been born out of insecurity. With Jenny, nothing ever lasted although the fault had lain with her. She had the male trait of being able to compartmentalise her life; love and sex were not the same thing. She ought to have been a man, he concluded, before walking over to the table which held his drinks and pouring another half-tumbler of Scotch.

He sat back in the brown leather settee which had altered its shape to suit his and speculated upon how Jenny could have antagonised someone enough to kill her. In Peter's mind there was no doubt it was murder. Jenny was no fool, apart from which she loved life. And, being so much a part of the place where she was born, she knew the dangers, she would not have been walking along perilous clifftops when the wind was off the land. Yes, she could be irritating, but so could most people. Revenge for an illicit love affair? It seemed unlikely in this day and age although men and women had been known to kill for less. No, Jenny may have been casual but she was careful and no one could accuse her of avarice. Initially it had crossed his mind that she may have stooped to blackmail but he soon saw how out of character this would have been. And as far as men were concerned, apart from one indiscretion with Daniel Wright, married men were not on her agenda. On the other hand Stella Jackson was an unknown quantity. She may well be financially independent of her husband and feminist enough to prefer to keep her own name but would she have tolerated an affair? Peter shook his head. It was highly unlikely she had found out. Nick Pascoe? he mused. No, too level-headed, he decided, and he had nothing to gain by it. Or had he? Had Jenny, who wanted him back, been making a nuisance of herself? And hadn't he occasionally sensed that violence lurked beneath the surface of Nick's urbanity?

He would miss Jenny and her contrary ways. As awkward as she could be at times, she still had had the capacity to mock herself and to make him laugh. Rumour had it that Nick was now seeing a woman from Newlyn, a fellow artist called Rose Trevelyan, one who, apparently, had allowed her talents to lie idle for too long. Naturally this might have upset Jenny but she was a fighter. It was six months since their relationship had ended but if she had set out to win Nick back, Peter doubted if the small matter of another woman would have troubled her.

In a couple of weeks he would meet this Mrs Trevelyan, possibly sooner if she was at Maddy's on the 26th. A widow. He grinned. 'You never know,' he said with a contented smile as he nudged the compact cylinder of ash off the end of his cigar with his little finger.

With his drink beside him he tried to calculate how long it would take the police to discover his relationship with Jenny. Perhaps, he concluded, they never would.

'Dead? She can't be dead.' Nick stared around the room as if it was strange to him or else the walls might provide the answer to what seemed like the present madness.

All three men were standing: himself, Inspector Pearce and another man whose name he had already forgotten. Despite the horror and outrage at what he had heard, Nick saw that some strong emotion also gripped the inspector beneath the grimness of his expression.

Jack Pearce was assessing his man, unsure how genuine the shock was. Everyone who had known Jenny would be interviewed although they would not yet be aware that this was a suspicious death. Her body had been found by a couple out walking. It had lain on the shoreline, her clothes and hair saturated, and the initial assumption had been that she had drowned. With the arrival of the police surgeon, a reliable man from Redruth, this had become less certain. He expressed his doubts and suggested that higher powers than his become involved. Jack had not digested the medical technicalities but had put the wheels in motion anyway. They had been lucky to find a pathologist to do the post-mortem early that afternoon. The police surgeon's suspicions had been confirmed. Jenny was dead before her body was immersed in water. Two blows to the back of the head had killed her. They had been barely detectable as the bleeding had stopped quickly in the icy salt water which had also washed away the blood. Her mass of hair had concealed the injuries which had not had time to swell. Tests on her lungs and stomach proved conclusively that she had not drowned.

A suspicious death, Jack thought, but not necessarily murder. There was the slim possibility that she had fallen, landed on rocks, then been washed out to sea and brought back to land when the current was right. It was unlikely, though. A fall serious enough to kill someone ought to have produced other injuries and there were none: no bruises or scratches anywhere else on her body. She had been dead for at least three days.

Nick Pascoe had been asked to make a formal statement. As her most recent lover and the man who had reported her missing, he was the obvious starting point, if not, Jack thought, the most obvious suspect in view of the fact that she had tried to revive their relationship.

Nick Pascoe had not been interested. Because of Rose? Jack asked himself.

And Rose knew these people, had known Jenny, and had been one of the last to see her alive. What sickened him was that she, too, had a motive. If she was desperate for Pascoe she might have felt the need to remove the younger, more attractive competition. Not that he believed that himself, Rose was far too pragmatic, but he knew how it might look to his colleagues. He could not protect her, she would have to be interviewed along with everyone else.

Those screams, what did they mean? Rose had reported them; Nick had reported Jenny, missing. Were they in something together?

Almost in imitation of Nick Pascoe, who was near to tears, Jack ran a hand through his thick, dark hair and sighed. He wanted nothing more than to go home and shower and get something to eat. But that luxury was hours away yet.

Stella Jackson was unaware of a conversation which had taken place between Daniel and Rose some weeks previously. Daniel had already forgotten it. He was not a man who had much recall when it came to things he had said.

'It's for the best, I think. Don't you agree? Under the circumstances,' she added with a touch of spite.

Daniel merely nodded. What a mess it all was. What a fool he had been. Thank goodness only the two of them knew. He was not a natural liar and neither was Stella but this he was more than necessary. They agreed to stick to the same story. The only person who could have invalidated their story was dead. Having listened to the news they knew it would not be long until the police arrived.

Rose stepped into her brightly lit kitchen, removed her raincoat and reached for the half-full bottle of wine she had opened for Laura the night before. It seemed more like a week ago. Then she lit a cigarette. Armed, as she called it, she went to the sitting room to listen to her messages, cheered by the chintz of her upholstery and the low lighting. She depressed the play button.

'Stella here. Will you ring me?' A bleep was followed by a second voice. 'Hi, it's Maddy. Your having a party gave me an idea. I'm having one Boxing Day afternoon. Do come. Let me know. Cheerio.'

About to erase the messages, she realised there had been a third call in her absence. 'It's Jack. Did you listen to the news? I can't talk now but I'll be in touch later.'

Rose knew he used the word later in the local way. It might mean this evening or any time during the next month. Am I up to returning these calls? she wondered, then decided she might as well in case people rang back when she was in bed. She longed for another early night and couldn't understand why she was so tired lately.

Stella answered on the second ring as if she had been hovering by the phone.

'I got your message,' Rose began.

'Have you heard?'

'About Jenny? Yes.'

'Isn't it awful? What on earth can have happened?'

106

Rose wished Stella hadn't bothered to contact her if all she wanted to do was speculate.

'And poor Maddy. She was the last one to see her alive. And to think she seemed fine when she left here.' Rose assumed she was now talking about Jenny. 'It's hard to imagine something like that happening while we were tucked up in our beds.'

'They didn't say when she died.'

'No, but it seems logical. Why else wasn't she seen after Thursday night? Anyway, don't let all this affect your work. You've got a long way to go yet.'

Rose made some excuse and hung up. It was true that things occurred in threes: the screams, the unknown woman in the shaft and now Jenny. Jenny had certainly been knocking back the drink at Stella's; if she had taken a walk along a cliff path she might have lost her footing, especially on the narrow muddy path. But it hadn't been raining then, Rose remembered. Stop it, she told herself. It isn't your problem. But something Stella had said was playing on her mind. 'When we were tucked up in our beds.' Surely Daniel had told her that Stella, nervous beforehand and wound up afterwards, always went for a long walk after a preview because she was unable to sleep. Rose shook her head. Stella was her mentor and an intelligent, highly talented woman. Why would she wish harm to an innocent girl? This is ridiculous, she thought. I don't even know how she died.

She felt a rumble of hunger. It was almost nine and time to think about food. As she opened cupboards it dawned on her that this would be her first Christmas alone. She planned to make it a hedonistic day, a day of small luxuries, and she would save her new novels until then.

Bone weary, her limbs feeling heavy, she had decided that scrambled eggs would have to suffice, but they would also have to wait. The phone rang again. It was Jack. At least he hadn't arrived in person. He, too, sounded exhausted and said he was ringing to warn her she would be required to make a statement.

'Yes, I was expecting to have to. Jack, does this mean what I think it means?'

'Rose, you know I can't . . .'

'Sorry. I shouldn't have asked.'

There was the slightest hesitation before he said, 'Maybe I could arrange to interview you myself. You knew them all.'

'They know each other better.'

'But they don't have your knack of seeing things that others don't.' This was not flattery. Rose had an eye for details, in what people said as well as in the way they looked. And she might be more formcoming with him than in a formal interview.

'When?'

'Soon. I'll let you know.'

Rose said goodnight and returned to the kitchen where she had got as far as cracking the eggs before she realised that, without actually saying so, Jack had let her know that Jenny Manders had been murdered. She threw the shells in the bin. I forgot to invite him to my party again, she thought, then wondered how she could possibly be thinking about such a thing after hearing the awful news.

\* \* \*

'Oh, don't, love.' Angela Choake, now Manders since they had married quietly in Penzance register office, sat down beside her husband and put her arm around his shoulders. She hated to see a man cry, especially one who was as outwardly tough as Alec. His body was firm, his muscles taut, and his face showed strength of character. She could not begin to imagine how he must feel because she had no children herself. She had not wanted them and this was one of the reasons her first marriage had ended. She did not like to admit that childbirth terrified her and she had had no intention of losing her figure.

Patting Alec's shoulder she got up and searched in the sideboard, unexpectedly finding some brandy. Alec rarely drank and his mother had not allowed alcohol in the house, or so he had told her in the days when their relationship had been a secret, although not as well-kept a secret as they had supposed. Probably the brandy was for medicinal purposes. Either way she needed it even if Alec refused it.

In the kitchen which her husband was in the process of modernising she fetched two glasses and poured generous measures, taking a sip from one of them before returning to the living room.

Alec wiped his eyes, blew his nose loudly and gave her a watery smile. With unexpected insight, Angela saw that he was confusing grief with guilt because he had largely ignored his daughter over the years. His mother had a lot to answer for: she had bound Alec to her with ties far stronger than apron strings and had prevented him from enjoying his marriage and loving Jenny.

Jenny was all right. From the little Angela knew of her

she had recognised her as a survivor despite the lack of affection from her small family.

After the passage of years it was hard to recall how their affair had come about. Angela supposed the attraction had been there from the day Alex came to fit a new sink at her old place. She had made him tea, aware that he struggled to keep his eyes from the contours of her body in tight-fitting jeans. It had been summertime and her large breasts, out of proportion to her figure, had pushed against the restraints of her T-shirt. Angela was striking rather than beautiful. She was aware that her face was quite ordinary but her figure could have belonged to the models who posed for top-shelf magazines and her long, straight red hair caused other heads to turn. She hoped no one realised that she now coloured it because the natural red was fading.

At forty-one and over a decade younger than Alec she still retained a carefree attitude to life. But only when her first marriage had ended had she really begun to enjoy life. Freed from the boredom of housekeeping and entertaining John's rather dry friends and their dull wives – whom, she suspected, he cultivated for these qualities because they provided a foil for his own charm and exuberance – she had started many projects, none of which had lasted. Finally she had taken a part-time job in a baker's where she still worked. Around the house she did as little as possible and spent the afternoons with friends or, in the summer, on the beach.

Alec was all that she wanted: a mixture of father, mother and lover. He could cook, he was tidy, far tidier than herself, and he was skilled with his hands which meant he could alter or repair anything in the house. Despite his rather stern demeanour and his lack of experience with women he was a good lover.

Watching him fighting back tears she felt a momentary disgust. It weakened him in her eyes because what she required from him was his particular maleness. She had no idea that what had attracted him was not so much her looks but her similarity to Agnes Manders, his mother. Angela was, without being aware of it, the head of the household and always managed to get her own way.

The police had come to break the news that Jenny was dead but they would be returning once Alec had had time to accept it. There were questions they needed to ask. Angela could not imagine her stepdaughter being stupid enough to go wandering over the cliffs at night, but maybe she had been drunk, maybe she was following in her mother's footsteps.

Alec had hardly tasted his drink but Angela's glass was empty. She refilled it in the kitchen hoping that he wouldn't notice. Running a finger over the smooth wood of the cupboards he had built for her she realised there would soon be no trace of the woman who had ruled this house for so many years once this last room had been modernised.

She frowned. Renata Manders had been a drinker. But had she been driven to it? If what she had heard about Agnes Manders was correct then it would not surprise her. But what am I doing now? she wondered as she stared at the dark gold liquid in her glass. Was there something about *Alec* that made women want to drink? It was a ridiculous idea, brought on by the shock she had received upon hearing of Jenny's death. But, as she stood in the still unfinished kitchen, she asked herself why, when they had both been free agents, she had gone along with his desire to keep their relationship a secret for so many years. For an independent woman it had been a strange way to behave. 'Is his attraction that strong?' she whispered. It was. She had never tired of his muscular body and his habit of saying little but thinking much. There was also the anomaly that, although he possessed an animal-like strength, it was Angela who was in control.

Well, she was his wife now and nothing could alter that. And she did not regret it either. Once the police had been back and the funeral was over life would revert to normal. They had nothing to fear.

Alec was not an intellectual man, he acted instinctively and only thought about what he had done afterwards. He did not know why he was crying, only that he was. His only child was dead but he hadn't loved her because he hadn't really known her. Odd, he thought, that he had not cried when his mother had died. But then, she would not have expected him to.

He had had no dealings with the police before and therefore no idea how they worked. Their questions would be answered, although there was little he could tell them about Jenny, and Angela, who had gone to Truro with a friend to see a film, did not know about Jenny's recent visit to the house. No one knew and there was no reason for them to do so. What had been discussed between father and daughter concerned them alone and the third party involved lived too far away for any connection to be made.

He gulped at the brandy. It burned unpleasantly but it did make him feel better.

Angela returned, a little flushed, her eyes over-bright. She sat beside him and took his hand in hers.

'I'm all right now,' he said. 'In fact, I think I'll plumb in the washing machine.'

Later that Monday night Angela gasped in surprise when Alec grabbed her before she was undressed and made love to her. It was as if she wasn't there. Normally their couplings were beneath the sheet and the duvet which had replaced Agnes Manders' scratchy blankets. Afterwards, he seemed at peace, as if by that one almost violent action he had got his daughter's death out of his system.

'Good evening, Inspector. Do come in.' Stella Jackson held open the plate glass door of the gallery, which had been closed for several hours. She ignored the sergeant at his side. Outside the Christmas lights glittered in the rain and were echoed in a much smaller way by the string of fairy lights on the minute tree in the corner of Stella's window. It was a sop to the season and did not detract from the carefully arranged display of her work. 'Shall we go upstairs? It's more comfortable.' The heating in the gallery went off at five-thirty and it was chilly.

Jack and his colleague followed the streamlined figure, tonight dressed entirely in black, up the spiral staircase. Stella Jackson reminded him of a sleek cat; a wild cat, he amended, although he could not say why the adjective had come to mind. Daniel Wright, the woman's husband, appeared in the doorway of the lounge as they approached.

The room took Jack by surprise with its tasteful uniqueness. He received another surprise when Daniel moved away and he saw the small figure of a woman sitting on the striped settee.

'This is Maddy Duke,' Stella said. 'Maddy, Inspector Pearce and, er . . . ?'

'Detective Sergeant Green,' Jack told her, thinking they might be able to kill two birds with one stone. Madeleine Duke was, apart from the killer, the last person to have set eyes on Jennifer Manders. As far as they knew. No one had come forward in response to the television and radio broadcasts but only hours had passed since the announcement. 'I know someone spoke to you at the time of Miss Manders' disappearance but I'm afraid it's necessary for us to go over the last time that you saw her again. I'm sure you're already aware of the news?' Maybe with three witnesses present one of them might jog another's memory. Some small fact, some forgotten line of dialogue could make all the difference.

'Yes. Of course we know. In a community this size . . .' Stella spread her hands. There was no need to finish the sentence. 'Sit down, Daniel, for goodness sake,' she snapped.

Jack observed her without seeming to. There were undercurrents here – had there been some disagreement between husband and wife? Was something troubling them? However, Maddy Duke appeared to be at ease so he had to assume the couple had not been in the middle of a blazing row immediately prior to their arrival.

The half-hour spent in the room over the gallery proved to be a waste of time. Jennifer Manders' three friends merely repeated what they had said when questioned about her disappearance; Stella and Daniel confirmed that she had been one of the last to leave. She had left alone and they had not noticed which direction she had taken. They had not seen her since. Stella, exhausted, had gone straight to bed and Daniel had made a half-hearted attempt at clearing up and followed her fifteen minutes later. Maddy had gone home earlier. She had not seen Jenny head towards Nick's place but had later observed her running down the hill, in a distressed state. Assuming she had come from Nick's she had telephoned to see if everything was all right. That was the last time she had seen Jenny. But later, although she did not say so, she had seen Nick walking in the same direction.

Jack wondered why Maddy was blushing. Was it the mention of Nick Pascoe's name? She had invited him for a meal, he recalled. Was he a womaniser? If so, he felt sorry for Rose. He thanked them for their time and noted their relief when he left. But he was far from satisfied. One or all of them were holding out on him.

It was just after nine on Tuesday morning when DS Green and a WPC turned up on Rose's doorstep. She heard the bell and frowned. The front door meant business. She struggled to pull it open, breaking a hail in the process, and wished she wasn't wearing her working clothes when she saw who her visitors were. She could hardly make a good impression in tattered jeans and a paint-splashed jumper. They refused the offer of coffee, which did not deter Rose from pouring one for herself before she joined them in the sitting room where she had shown them.

It was soon established how long and how well she had known Jenny, which was no more than a few months and hardly at all.

'Mrs Trevelyan, it is our understanding that you've been seeing Nicholas Pascoe. Were you aware he had been in a longstanding relationship with Miss Manders?'

'Yes, I was.'

'And that, recently, she decided she wanted this relationship to resume?'

'Yes.'

'I see. How did you feel about that?'

'I didn't think much about it, really. Nick said it was over and that he wasn't interested in renewing it.'

'And you believed him?'

'I had no reason not to. Besides, although I see him, as you put it, he's no more than a friend.' But Rose got the feeling that they did not believe *her*.

'Forgive my asking, but were you jealous of Miss Manders?'

Rose stared at the detective, her eyes wide. Then she laughed but wished she hadn't. She was being too flippant. 'Of course not. I liked her, in fact. Anyway, I knew their affair was over. Other people confirmed it, too.'

'You needed confirmation?'

Rose was annoyed. Sergeant Green was no fool but he was beginning to make her look one. 'No, I didn't actually ask anyone, it just came up in conversation. Gossip, if you like.'

'Yet on the night Miss Jackson held her preview Miss Manders was present, along with Mr Pascoe, and later she

turned up at his house. They were obviously still friends.'
Before Rose could speak he continued, 'When you left the
gallery where did you go?'

'I came straight home.'

'And later Mr Pascoe telephoned. Did you know Miss
Manders was with him at the time?'

'No. Not then.' Rose closed her mouth. Not then? Not
at all, she thought. He certainly hadn't mentioned it. But
she had heard the knock on the door and subconsciously
registered that it was probably Jenny. But why? Rose
frowned in concentration.

Because of the flirtatious way in which Jenny had been
behaving at the gallery, she realised.

DS Green was relentless. 'Who might have seen you
after you left St Ives?'

'No one. I told you, I came straight home.'

'So we only have your word for it that you didn't go out
again that night after you received the telephone call.' It
was a statement.

'Yes, you only have my word for it,' she replied with
resignation.

DS Green leant back in his chair. It was his colleague's
turn now. WPC Sanderson had a flawless face with
a mask-like expression. Her looks were classic but
cold. 'Miss Manders was young and beautiful – some
competition, I'd say.'

Rose's mouth fell open. She was speechless. She had
never thought in those terms. More so than ever she wished
she looked smarter. Surely she wasn't as bad as all that?

'All right, Mrs Trevelyan, let's move on to those screams

you claimed to have heard. What were you doing out at the mine?'

'Painting.' Rose knew that whatever she said she would end up under suspicion.

'Inspector Pearce thinks there might be a connection between the death of Miss Manders and the body recovered from the mine. And, for whatever reason, you seem to have become involved with both of these women.'

'But I'm not. I had no idea there was a body there. How could I have done?'

'Perhaps the screams were in your imagination. Perhaps it was your way of telling us we ought to investigate.'

'That's a bloody stupid theory.' She was angry. How dare Jack have allowed this situation to have arisen. Hadn't he told her he would interview her himself?

WPC Sanderson raised her eyebrows sardonically. Rose thought her too smug for her own good. 'Maybe someone *did* know what was down there and the screams were meant to scare me away. Look, I can't explain why you didn't find anybody there at the scene but I definitely heard them. Could they have been recorded?' Rose asked doubtfully.

Her question was ignored. 'When did you move here?'

Rose was shaken. 'About twenty-eight years ago,' she said.

WPG Sanderson stood and gestured for her colleague to do the same. Her cat-like smile was explicit in its meaning. Rose had been around when the woman in the mine shaft had died. 'Thank you, Mrs Trevelyan, that'll be all for now.' DS Green nodded a farewell as his colleague followed him out into the hall. Rose let him open the front door himself.

'Right! Work,' she said with determination but before she could leave the house Nick telephoned.

'God, Rose, what a mess. It seems I'm a suspect.'

'Well; don't think you're so special. So am I.'

'You?' He started to laugh then realised just why she might be considered so.

'Older, jealous woman removes the obstacle to her happiness,' she said bitterly.

Nick was uncertain exactly what she meant by this. Did she feel more for him than her manner suggested? Did she want him that much? 'I'm sure they don't . . .'

'They do. Nick, when exactly did Jenny turn up at your place that night?' Rose suddenly realised she had, if not lied, then been economical with the truth. She did not know that Jenny had been there when Nick telephoned, she had, she realised, only guessed as much.

'After the preview. I told you.'

'Before or after you rang me?'

'Hey, what is this? As we were talking, actually. I wasn't expecting her. Why do you want to know?'

'No reason, really. Just curiosity.'

'Anyway, I know you're busy but is there any chance . . . ?'

'No, Nick. Let's leave it until Saturday as arranged.'

'Okay. You're the boss. I'll see you then.'

His disappointment sounded genuine but Rose did have other things to do. Work, for a start, and she needed time to think about all that had occurred over the past few days.

She got into the car and found herself heading towards St Ives. She could not stop thinking that it was Nick who had had the perfect opportunity of following Jenny after she had left his place. Or Stella, she thought. But no, not Stella. Maybe she really had gone to bed. She had looked very tired.

It was another fine day, but chilly. Rose's hair, left loose, flew around her face when she got out of the car. In her uniform of jeans, shirt, sweatshirt and waxed jacket she made her way towards what was locally called the island although it was joined to the mainland. Her route took her past Stella's gallery.

Stella was behind the counter, some paperwork spread out in front of her. Daniel, dressed smartly in trousers, shirt, jacket and tie, was on the telephone. Both looked pale, as if they had not slept much.

'Rose. Nice to see you.' Stella looked up when the door opened. Her eyes shifted to the canvas bag over Rose's shoulder. 'Are you over here to work?'

'Yes.'

'I thought you'd be more adventurous. Absolutely everyone's had a bash at painting St Ives.'

Rose ignored the comment. 'Have the police been to see you?'

'Yes. Last night. We weren't able to be much help, I'm afraid. Do you get the feeling they think someone killed her? Perhaps it was a lover. She wasn't too fussy when it came to men.'

Shocked at such callousness so soon after Jenny's death, Rose was still aware of the odd look which was exchanged between husband and wife. The tell-tale flush spreading along Daniel's high cheekbones confirmed what Rose already suspected. Jenny had had an affair with Daniel

Wright. Did Jack know? Well, it's up to him to find out, she thought, she was in enough trouble as it was. And did Jack know that Stella went walking after previews? No wonder the pair of them appeared anxious, she thought, if they weren't together it gives them both a motive: Stella's being jealousy, Daniel's the threat of being found out. It was crazy to be suspecting her friends, but perhaps no more crazy than the police suspecting her.

'Rose? I said, would you like a coffee?'

'Oh, no thanks, Stella, I've got a flask. I just called in as I was passing.' What's happening to me, she thought as she left the gallery. It's as if I don't trust anyone. She blamed it on the circumstances. Murder was ugly and its repercussions spread like ripples in widening circles of doubt and suspicion.

Once on the island Rose got to work, one eye on the sky as she waited for the weather to decide what to do. Grey clouds blew in from the sea then dispersed again and the threatened rain was held at bay because of the speed with which they scudded overhead. Despite the fingerless gloves in which she worked, Rose's hands were cold and stiff. She gave it up as a bad job, dissatisfied with what she had produced but not unduly upset as she had already seen ways in which it could be improved.

Gulls swirled in noisy flocks as she made her way down the grassy slope. On a high, jutting rock a black-back, neck stretched, sharp curved beak open, squawked noisily. Beneath her lay St Ives, peaceful on a winter's afternoon without the clutter of cars and tourists the season would bring. Herring-gulls lined the harbour wall, facing the wind, their feathers unruffled. They cocked their heads to watch her as she passed, each with one bright eye visible, assessing whether she was a danger to them, but they did no more than take a couple of sideways steps. These scavengers were used to people.

Rose had known all along what she intended doing but only now admitted it to herself. But was it the right thing to do? She was being presumptuous. She grinned. Barry Rowe would have certainly thought so. She pulled her hair from the confines of the collar of her jacket and walked on. But Barry Rowe isn't here to see me, she told herself.

She knew the street in which Alec Manders lived because Jenny had mentioned it, but not the number. It was Maddy who had filled her in on Jenny's childhood. Rose could not imagine what it must have been like to have a mother abandon you at an age when her presence was so necessary. Rose's own upbringing had been totally secure. Maybe that was why David's death had hit her so hard – she had taken security for granted. No, it wasn't that. It was because I loved him in a way I'll never be able to love any other human being, she decided. And with that thought she felt better about doubting Nick. She knew her feelings for him would never be as deep.

The street, like many others, was wide enough to allow only one car to pass because it had been built at a time when horses and carts dragged boxes of pilchards and other fish along the roads which wound steeply up from the harbour. The front doors opened directly on to the pavement.

Two women stood talking but paused in their conversation to eye her curiously as she approached them.

'Can you tell me where Alec Manders lives?' she asked with a smile.

'That's his place, there.' The one wearing a tightly knotted headscarf pointed diagonally across the road, avid inquisitiveness unconcealed in both her demeanour and her expression.

'The one with the plant pots?'

'Ess.' The woman nodded emphatically. 'What do 'ee want with 'en?'

'Thank you.' Rose smiled again, fully aware of their disappointed silence and their eyes on her back as she walked up the street.

The plant pots were stacked on the stone steps at the side of the building. They contained only dead things. Rose knocked and the door was answered by a woman younger than herself who smiled welcomingly and said, yes, Alec was at home.

Rose stepped over the threshold and smelt new wood and fresh paint.


Maddy Duke had a job to concentrate as she gave change to customers. In the run-up to Christmas the shop was doing well.

She felt unsettled. Stella was keeping something from her, she sensed it, and Nick was being evasive. It was beginning to get to all of them. Yet she could not bring herself to feel sorry that Jenny was dead. Watching her, distraught, running away from the direction in which Nick's house lay, Maddy knew what had happened. Jenny had tried to seduce him. Her remarks about Rose Trevelyan earlier that evening had not gone unheeded although Maddy could see that there wasn't much doing there. At least, not yet. Nor would there be if she had her way.

It was peculiar really because she had liked Jenny and she liked Rose. She hated herself for the ambiguity she felt towards her friends, liking but envying them. In Nick's case she wanted him badly but she also wanted her freedom, to have no ties if Annie should seek her out. She had invited Peter Dawson to accompany her in the hope of making Nick jealous. But now she was worried. What had Nick been doing that night? And, more to the point, had anyone seen her hurrying through the deserted streets? She wondered if she even cared.

Perhaps the way she was stemmed from the past, from the loss of her child, the one thing she really wanted and could not have. Even though her prayers would be answered if her daughter made contact when she reached her eighteenth birthday early next year, she would never be able to retrieve the years of her babyhood and childhood. There would be no compensation for that.

When she had closed the shop she went upstairs to study the script for the Christmas pantomime although she was almost word perfect. She had joined the drama group as a way of overcoming her lack of confidence as well as to make new friends. At first she had been rejected at every audition and had had to settle for helping with costumes and scenery but once she had begun to tape, in secret, the voices of her friends she had tried to copy them and had eventually become a good mimic. She had finally landed a decent part because she could now speak in voices other than her own accentless one.

On the stage she could become someone else but no one knew how far she carried this over into her real life. And certainly no one knew of her small collection of tapes on which were recorded the voices of her friends in conversation.

# CHAPTER SIX

'It's not much to go on.' Inspector Jack Pearce hooked his thumbs in his trouser pockets and leant his large frame against the windowsill in his office. The results, so far, of the examination of the bones of the female found in the shaft showed that she was white, of average height and build and aged somewhere between twenty-one and thirty-five. There was no jewellery, no remnants of a handbag, nothing at all to suggest who the woman was. This added to the likelihood that she had been murdered.

Jack walked to his desk and read upside down, as if to confirm what he already knew. He tapped the top sheet of paper. 'And that's all we needed to know.'

The only other occupant of the room was a grizzled sergeant, more astute than his amenable manner and gentle expression suggested. He knew Jack was referring to the dental report. All the woman's teeth were her own and there wasn't a trace of amalgam. Whoever it was had lain there for twenty-five to thirty-five years but the computer file which held the information regarding missing persons had not come up with anyone who fitted the flimsy description. The few who came closest had reappeared or had been found elsewhere somewhere along the line, either living or dead. He knew Jack had also gone to the trouble of checking an extra five years either side of the margins given them by Forensics.

Jack was baffled. A holidaymaker, even if alone, would have left some trace of herself. There would be unclaimed belongings in her accommodation, no matter how lowly or grand, and there would, presumably, be the matter of an unpaid bill. On the other hand, someone local would certainly have been missed. He hoped that the abruptly curtailed life had not belonged to some lonely individual with no one to care whether they had lived or died; someone who had come to the area with the sole purpose of ending it all. If that was the case her identity might remain a mystery for ever. But Jack had a feeling it was vitally important to know who she was.

For now there was the more pertinent case of Jennifer Manders. He needed to speak to the dead girl's father. She had been dead only a few days and therefore there was still a good chance of apprehending her killer. The other woman, whose death might yet turn out to be accidental, had waited twenty-odd years for someone to take an interest. A little while longer couldn't hurt.

Oh, Rose, he thought, as he went out to the car. Why on earth did you have to become involved? On the other hand, without her involvement they would not have found the anonymous female. He headed towards St Ives where Alec Manders had been told to expect him, praying that Rose would not get herself into deeper trouble.

\* \* \*

Almost the same thought was going through her own mind as Rose chewed the ends of her hair, a childhood habit her mother thought she had cured but which recurred when she was deep in thought. She needed someone to talk to, someone to whom she could voice her suspicions aloud, but the most suitable listener was Jack, and he had too much else on his plate to spare her any time. Not that she had asked him to.

She glanced at her watch – six-thirty – but rang his number anyway, surprised when he answered in person. 'I've just this minute got home,' he told her. He was tired and disappointed at the outcome of his interview with Manders.

It was some time since Rose had been to his flat in Morrab Road but she could picture it clearly. It was on the ground floor, one of two into which a solid-looking house had been converted. He had moved there after his wife had returned to Leeds, taking with her their two sons. They were men now and had always visited Jack regularly; the divorce was a thing of the past.

Jack, having yearned for experience away from the area, had been transferred and had met and married his wife in Yorkshire. When the boys were small he had moved back, drawn to his roots as were most Cornishmen if far from home for any length of time. His wife had been unable to settle. There was no chance of a compromise; Jack's wife refused to stay and Jack refused to leave again.

'I've decided to throw a party on New Year's Eve. Will you come, Jack?'

The way she said his name still gave him a strange

sensation in his stomach. He thought about it then smiled wryly. 'Will I get a kiss at midnight?'

'If you're exceptionally well behaved you might.' But she had to warn him. 'The St Ives lot will be there, you know, Nick and everyone.'

'Ah.'

'And the Clarkes, Doreen and Cyril. Remember them? And Laura and her family, and Barry, of course.'

'I should hope so. The sycophantic Mr Rowe would cut his wrists if he didn't receive an invitation.'

Rose stiffened. Was he being sarcastic or gently mocking? If she could have seen his face she would have known it was the latter. It was true, though, Barry would have monopolised her if she had not been firm. However, if Rose ran him down silently now and then, that was one thing, but she was completely loyal to her friend and would not allow anyone else to do so. 'He's a kind, decent man, Jack, and a very good friend to have.'

'Sorry, Rose. I know that. And he succeeds in those things without trying.'

She had no idea what he meant but she was more intent on finding out if he was coming to the party. 'You still haven't said, will you be here?'

'Can you put me down as a maybe? It all depends, you see.'

'Of course.' Rose understood it might be awkward for all concerned as Jack would have already interviewed some of her guests, might even, she realised, have arrested one of them by then.

'Thanks for asking.'

Rose had wanted to talk to him but sensed that he was anxious to get off the phone. She said goodbye and hung up with a shrug. Her amateur detection work would have to wait. 'Really, Mrs Trevelyan, this won't do,' she told herself. 'Seven o'clock and no wine opened.'

This remedied, she put a casserole in the oven to reheat then sat at the kitchen table doodling on a piece of paper. Rose stared at what she had written; the names Nick Pascoe, Stella Jackson, Daniel Wright and Maddy Duke, in that order. Maddy? Despite the animosity she had felt between Maddy and Jenny on that one occasion there was no reason to think she might have killed her. Then Rose remembered the pointed remarks concerning herself and Nick. What was going on there? And Maddy hadn't wasted any time in ringing Nick to confirm that Jenny had been with him after Stella's preview.

'Oh, no.' Suddenly Rose saw it clearly. Maddy wanted Nick for herself. How far would she have gone to get him? I was blind not to see it before, she thought. And Maddy was an actress. Had she been there at the mine and given those screams, throwing her voice in some way, or whatever it was called? But why? And what relevance did it have to the remains found there or Jenny's death?

Alec Manders, she wrote next, alongside the list. Not because she thought he was a suspect but because the written name helped to bring him closer. He had been touched rather than annoyed or upset at her visit and had recalled, without prompting, meeting her that day with Jenny and the fact that she was an artist. Rose had been flattered, and glad that she had called to offer her condolences. She knew from experience that it helped in the months to come, that comfort was taken from the kind words of friends and people whom you hardly knew. It had taken her a long time to realise how hard these words were to say, that the platitudes were meant despite being what they were – how else could anyone really express what they felt for the bereaved? And how much easier it was to ignore the one suffering.

At least he has Angela, Rose thought. And they did seem well suited, comfortable together, if an unlikely pair. From the little Rose knew of him via Jenny and Maddy she had gained the impression that Alec expected people living under his roof to obey him. Angela, however, appeared to have made him more biddable and had an air of being able to do more or less as she pleased.

Alec had been more open with Rose than she had anticipated. She was a virtual stranger, but that might have made it easier for him to talk, especially as she saw him as a man who did not waste words. But Rose was unaware that the brandy, which he was not used to, had loosened his tongue.

She ran a hand through her hair, tangled by the wind because she had left it loose. A faint smell of meat and vegetables escaped from the oven and made her mouth water but the casserole would not be hot enough yet.

With only the hum of the fridge and the low buzzing of the fluorescent tube for company, Rose sipped a second glass of wine.

Did Renata Trevaskis, or Manders, or whatever she might now be calling herself, know that the daughter she had abandoned was dead? Alec Manders had more or less told her the same thing as Maddy. Renata had taken to drink and running around with other men and had finally run off altogether with one of them. Alec had received one letter giving little more information than her address.

'I don't know why she bothered,' he said to Rose, 'she never wrote again, not even to the child. Still, it saved a lot of trouble when it came to the divorce. The solicitors needed to know where to write and to advise her to get her own lawyer.'

After a six-year separation there had been no need for either party to attend court. There were no objections on either side and Renata had made no claim upon his money. She had also admitted that she had not set foot in the marital home during that time and that she had been cohabiting with someone else. He had told her all this spontaneously, as if glad to have an opportunity to talk about the past. It was noticeable that he had chosen to do so whilst Angela was out of the room.

Alec's face had hardened when Rose asked if Jenny's mother would be attending the funeral. She got the impression that Renata didn't know. But perhaps after such a long time she had moved from the original address given and Alec had been unable to locate her.

The kitchen was becoming very warm. Rose turned off the gas, slipped on her oven gloves and, momentarily backing away from the blast of heat as she opened the oven door, bent her knees to reach for the smoked-glass dish with its bubbling contents.

She realised she was starving, which was a good sign, and

looked forward to a slice of Doreen Clarke's home-made saffron cake afterwards. It was rich in colour and full of fruit, and she would spread it generously with butter.

Nick Pascoe was more worried than his friends knew. He had been on edge ever since Jenny had disappeared and he knew it didn't look good for him. He had lied to the police and he had lied to Rose. And although Maddy was the last known person to have seen Jenny alive as far as the police were concerned, he knew better. But he was in any case the last person known to have spoken to her. And he had made no secret of the fact that they had argued.

Rose seemed to have cooled towards him but whether this was because she was upset over Jenny's death or because she had heard what he had tried to keep from her, he didn't know. Maybe she was simply hurt because Jenny had been with him that night. At least she hadn't dropped him altogether. He knew little of Rose's past, only that she had been married, happily married, but the name Jack Pearce had cropped up often enough for Nick to have drawn the correct conclusion. If his assessment of her was accurate, Rose was a truthful, open and sensible woman, and certainly not prone to histrionics as Jenny had been. But he still couldn't bring himself to tell her the truth.

On Wednesday, unable to concentrate, Nick mooched about the bedroom he used as his studio for most of the long, wet day, assessing his work and finally choosing the last two paintings for the exhibition. The rain hammered on the corrugated iron roof of the bathroom extension below him. Less than thirty years ago these cottages had only had a stone sink with a cold tap in the kitchen. An outside lavatory had once stood at the end of each small back yard but since the modernisation of the row they now acted as storage sheds.

Normally Nick found the sound of rain soothing: today its constant staccato beat in time with his jumping nerves. The telephone receiver sat quietly on its cradle, although most of his friends knew he rarely answered it when he was working and left their calls until after six. Today he could have done with some company. His hands were shaking and did not feel as though they belonged to him. Angrily, he pulled on a leather jacket, closed the door of the cottage and walked down the hill to the harbour. The tide was out. A few small boats lay at an angle waiting to be righted by the incoming tide. The fine wet sand lay in hard rippled ridges in which herring-gulls left their footprints as they stalked aggressively across them. Far out to sea a beam-trawler cut through the swell, white spray sweeping over its bows. It would dip and roll a lot more once it was further out to sea. The smell of brine was mingled with that of wet tarpaulin and frying onions from one of the cafes. With his hands in his pockets Nick walked around as far as the lighthouse, breathing deeply as if he could clear the clutter in his mind. The rain was heavier than he had realised. His jeans clung to his legs stiffly and chafed. He ought to go home.

In dry clothes he stood by the telephone, hesitating before dialling Rose's number. She might be working and he would feel bad if he disturbed her. She had made it clear she was not prepared to see him before the weekend. Three times he lifted the receiver, three times he decided against calling her.

What the hell's wrong with me? Nick thought. It's more than Jenny and more than the weather and I'm acting like a petulant child. It struck him that he might be just that, albeit in an adult body. No attempt had ever been made to curb his selfish streak. He also had a deep-seated fear that he wasn't quite up to the mark and this caused him either to withdraw or to behave badly towards people whom he liked.

Although he was lucky enough to have been recognised during his lifetime he was far from sure his talent would outlive him. Which was worse? To die unknown then become famous when it was too late to matter, or to fear that your life's work would be forgotten once you were no longer around?

He did try to minimise the violent mood swings from which he suffered but perhaps other artists also underwent periods of self-doubt followed by bursts of euphoria. Could Rose Trevelyan cope with his moods? More to the point, could he cope with her? He was not used to her total independence and straightforward ways. Being the sort of man who, when he wanted something, had to have it immediately also meant the reverse applied. He was capable of rejecting whatever he had desired just as quickly. Jenny had not been malleable, far from it, but in retrospect Nick saw that he had been so busy double-guessing her that his own feelings had been put on hold.

Nick was an enigma to himself. He was unable to decide if his discontent came from getting too much or too little out of life. At the moment, as far as women were concerned, he seemed to be getting far too much. Maddy's visit that morning had disturbed him greatly and was too reminiscent of Jenny's last one. It was a mystery how he attracted such behaviour. Maddy Duke was obviously disturbed and had a deep-seated envy of Jenny. It was strange that he had never noticed this before. And now he had further cause for anxiety. Maddy had seen him on the night of Jenny's death. If he didn't go along with her wishes she might well go to the police.

Maddy had risen early, long before daylight. After a restless night she had come to a decision. She knew that Nick was an insomniac and guessed that he would also be up and about.

There was no point in opening the shop until ten, few people had fancy goods on their mind that early in the day. However, she rang the girl who helped out occasionally if Maddy wanted a few hours off and she agreed to open up. She had a spare set of keys. Maddy had finally had to trust someone and in Sally's case she had not been let down. Working a six-day week, seven in the height of the season, it was essential to have some assistance even if it did cut into her profits.

In the darkness she passed few people and no one she knew. She had not set eyes on Nick for several days but since Jenny's death none of them seemed to be communicating as much as usual. It was a shame, but nothing could compare to the loss of little Annie. No, not little, she reminded herself. A young woman now. The bitterness was always with her and she suspected it always would be. Stella had pointed out how well she had done for herself but had managed to make it more like an insult when she spoke of 'your little business'. But success wasn't enough. She wanted, not as most people seemed to, someone to love her, but someone whom she could love. At times she thought she could settle for simply being accepted as one of the crowd. Deep down she realised that this could not be. Not because she was neither Cornish nor an artist but because there was a barrier between herself and others, one of her own construction.

Layers of clothing disguising her reasonable body, Maddy set off up the hill. To see Nick, to hear his voice, would be balm to her miserable state. Hard as she tried to conquer these spells of depression there were some which were undefeatable.

As far as she could discern, he was not getting very far with Rose. This pleased her. And now that Jenny was no longer around Maddy was sure she could persuade Nick that she would be good for him. I can make him happy, I know I can, she told herself.

She slowed her pace to take the steep incline up to his house. Lights showed in the windows and the door was ajar. Nick always liked plenty of fresh air whatever the time of year. She rapped her knuckles on the weather-roughed wood of the door and called his name.

'Come in, Maddy. I'm in the kitchen.'

Already feeling more cheerful at his welcoming tone, she went through, picking her way amongst the general untidiness of the room where books and papers and picture frames were scattered. Nick was standing by the sink. She saw at once that lack of sleep was plaguing him again. The skin beneath his eyes looked bruised and the lines in his face more deeply etched. 'Are you all right, Nick?' she asked.

'Yes. Just can't sleep, dammit. It'll pass.'

'There's nothing worrying you, is there?' Maddy kept her voice light, hoping that Rose Trevelyan was not the cause of his sleeplessness.

'No, nothing apart from Jenny and that's hanging over all our heads.'

'Would you like me to make you some breakfast?' she had asked.

'What about the shop?'

'Sally's opening up for me. I just felt like an hour or two away from it all. It's been satisfyingly busy. Breakfast then?' She smiled widely, showing her neat white teeth.

'Food might be a good idea, actually. But only if you join me.'

It was a pleasure to be allowed the run of his kitchen although she had to open all the cupboards and drawers to find things. Nick ignored her, his mind elsewhere. How nice it would be if I could do this every day, she thought while she boiled the kettle and poached eggs as there was little else in the fridge. She fantasised that she was already living with Nick, that they would become an accepted couple. It was a shame he was so tired, his problems should be over now that Jenny wasn't hanging around his neck. Their relationship may have been over as far as Nick was concerned but Jenny had had other ideas. She had confided in Maddy that she was determined to get him back, hinting that it was never really over. Jenny had said something else, too, but for the moment Maddy couldn't recall the rest of the conversation. 'I can live with his moods,' Jenny had said, laughing. 'My God, I ought to be able to after all that time. He doesn't know what he wants, that's his problem. It takes a woman to show him. You'll see, I'll soon be moving back in.'

Maddy had doubted that very much. But now she realised that what Jenny had said may have held some truth. She *had* known him well. Perhaps it was time that she, Maddy, showed Nick what he wanted; namely, herself. The trouble was, she suspected, that they had met as friends and he was unable to see her as a desirable woman.

'It's ready.' Maddy carried the warm plates to the scarred wooden kitchen table and placed salt and pepper in the middle. Two eggs each, on thick slices of buttered toast. Steaming mugs of tea were at the sides of their plates.

Nick ate as if he was ravenous and she wondered if he was looking after himself.

'That's better. Food always tastes nicer when someone else cooks it.'

Maddy beamed. These were the sort of words she lived to hear. 'I love cooking,' she said. 'Come for dinner tonight, why don't you? I've got all morning to find us something special.'

'Thanks, Maddy, but I'll probably turn in early. I'm so damned tired.'

Her face fell but she was determined not to let her disappointment show. A tirelessly cheerful companion was what Nick needed. Then she thought of another way to help him relax. Slowly she cleared the table and washed the dishes in the old stone sink. 'Fancy another cup of tea?' she inquired artlessly, wanting to stay as long as possible.

'Yes, I do. Thanks.'

'Go and sit down, for goodness sake, Nick, before you fall down.' Jenny was right, Maddy thought, Nick only needs to be told what to do. She took the tea into the living room, pleased to note that he was on the settee, and joined him there. They sipped it and Maddy asked him about his painting and what he was working on. When both mugs were empty she moved a little closer to him and reached for his hand, stroking the back of his roughened fingers gently. When he did not resist she brought her left hand around to his chest. Not until her hand was beneath his jumper and unbuttoning his shirt did Nick seem to realise her intentions.

'Maddy, don't.'

'Why not? Surely you like it.'

'Leave me alone, for God's sake.' He jumped up and stalked into the kitchen.

Maddy followed him. 'I just want to help, Nick, to make things right for you. I'll take care of you, I promise. Please believe me.' She was desperate. 'You have to believe me. I didn't tell the police I saw you, after all.'

'What?' Nick spun round. 'What're you talking about?'

'On the night Jenny died. I saw you. You were following her.'

'You're mistaken. How could I have been following her when I was on the phone to you?'

'Not immediately. But not all that long after she left.'

'It wasn't me,' Nick shouted. 'It wasn't me, you stupid

141

bitch.' He left by the back door of the house, slamming it hard behind him.

Tears filled Maddy's eyes and her face was hot with shame and humiliation. She wanted to run and hide but she also wanted to stay, to ask him what was so wrong with her that he couldn't bear her to touch him. When he didn't return after a few minutes she left quietly and walked slowly down the hill. Reaching the bottom she turned left and began to run as suppressed rage boiled up within her. It's Rose's fault, she thought, Rose Trevelyan with her girlish figure and her bloody talent.

It was not yet nine-thirty. Maddy knew the only release would be to return to the shop and work, to make an effort to be pleasant to the customers. As soon as she returned she rang Sally to say that her services weren't needed then she cried until she felt there were no more tears to be shed. By the time Rose walked into the shop around lunch time she was more or less her normal self. The permanent ache she felt was still there but she realised her behaviour could hardly have endeared her to Nick. And she had had time to wonder just what he really had been doing that night.

Rose hated being under suspicion, hated the whole idea of Jenny's death and the way everyone had been affected, but at least she had worked out her next move. She was going to see Maddy, using the excuse of buying Barry's Christmas present for being in the shop. It was not even out of her way as she had arranged to meet Stella that afternoon. If it wasn't raining they would go for a walk. Stella hated the rain. Rose intended making the most of the opportunity by asking advice on holding her own exhibition and, if she was really lucky, persuading Stella to allow her to do so in her gallery.

The sky was dull but Rose decided to dress smartly in deference to her hostess. She put on an olive green skirt and a cream lambswool sweater then, after a leisurely breakfast, left the house, for once having read more than the front page of the newspaper.

St Ives was busy. Panic buying, she thought, and so much of it would go to waste. The narrow streets were crowded although Truro, Plymouth and Exeter were the places which benefited most at that time of year. As yet, apart from the awful superstores on the edge of Penzance, there were none of the big stores in the area. Rose preferred the small shops, run by individuals rather than by faceless men who sat around boardroom tables.

She walked down the hill, stepping off the narrow pavement every so often to pass slower, window-gazing pedestrians. Light spilt from the shops making the sky seem duller than it really was. The mouth-watering aroma of freshly cooked pasties wafted into the streets as she passed the various bakers'. Decorations glowed and even Rose began to feel festive.

A bell tinkled as she pushed open the door of Maddy's shop. There were already three other customers browsing. Maddy had stacked every surface with goods. Two women and one man handled objects as they decided whether or not to buy them. The whole gamut of Maddy's talents filled the shelves and the tables down the centre of the room. It was hard to know where to look first with so many brightly coloured articles to catch the eye. Mobiles swirled overhead, moved by the warm air of the fan-heater behind the counter, and silver bells tinkled. There were painted wooden toys, drawn-threadwork table linen, ceramics and papier mache containers. Not wishing to draw attention to herself until they were alone, Rose kept her back to the counter where Maddy was writing a receipt for one of the women and had a good look around. Rose and her friends had given up sending one another cards many years ago. It seemed so pointless when they were in daily contact. Those few she did send had already been posted. Laura was often broke so she and Rose had made a pact years ago only to buy one another something inexpensive, a token. The only other gifts she bought now were for her parents and Barry, although she had made an exception last year and bought Jack a bottle of his favourite malt and framed a sketch of hers he had admired.

On a shelf, Rose spotted what she took to be a pen-holder, shaped and hollowed from a single piece of wood whose legend claimed it came from the wreck of a ship. The outside was rough, the wood grained and interesting, but inside it had been squared out smoothly. Six inches high and with a firm heavy base, it would act as one even if that was not what it was intended for. She peered at the sticky label which displayed the price. Five pounds. She would take it.

'Bye, and thanks,' she heard Maddy say as the shop door bell jangled again. 'Rose, I didn't see you come in. Need any help?'

'No, thanks. I'm going to have this, but I'm still looking.'

Maddy went back to serve an elderly woman with bow

legs and an old-fashioned wicker basket which contained a Yorkshire terrier.

'It's good to be so busy,' Maddy commented when the shop was empty at last. 'Four fifty to you,' she added, tilting the wooden object to check the price. Her need to be liked was greater than her envy of Rose.

'Thank you. But I really didn't come expecting a discount.'

'What're friends for? Fancy a coffee and a sandwich? I'm closing for lunch. It's too long a day otherwise.'

Rose looked at her watch. There was plenty of time before she was due to meet Stella. 'Thanks, I'd love a coffee.'

There was nothing else she wanted to buy. For her parents, who claimed to have everything they needed at their time of life, Rose had ordered a hamper of food to be sent. It contained only Cornish produce: hog's pudding, clotted cream, pasties, fudge, saffron cake, ginger fairings and heavy cake. There was also a small box of salted pilchards. Enclosed with their card she had sent a recipe book in case her mother decided to try her hand at baking any of the cakes, and an explanation to go along with the heavy cake. 'Folklore says it goes back to biblical times,' she had written. 'It's also known as "fuggan" and was eaten by the "hewer" and somehow got its name from the cry of "hewa" which he'd shout from his look-out in the days when men were employed to watch for the shoals of fish, pilchards mostly, from a vantage point on the cliffs. Anyway, enjoy it, it's delicious, especially if you warm it up.'

Maddy locked the door and turned the sign to closed

then led Rose out through the back and up a flight of uncarpeted stairs to her flat.

'Did you make everything in the shop?' Rose inquired.

'Yes. Well, most of it. I'm a real Jack-of-all-trades.'

'Amazing. Anyway, I'm really pleased with my find. It's for Barry Rowe, do you know him?'

'Does he run that greeting-card place in Penzance?'

'That's him. He produces all his own stuff too. All done by local artists.'

'Good for him. I don't actually know him, only the shop because his name's over the door.'

Rose had been about to comment that the pen-holder was an ideal present for a man who was so disorganised then realised Maddy might be offended if that was not its purpose. Although the desk in Barry's small office behind the shop was piled high with paperwork there was never a pen to be found.

'Have a seat.' Maddy indicated the over-stuffed chairs and a small sofa. The room was cluttered but not untidy. It made Rose a little claustrophobic.

'I won't be long. Ham okay?'

'Just coffee for me, Maddy, really.' She hesitated, then came straight to the point as Maddy turned in the kitchen doorway. 'I didn't come only to buy a present. Maddy, I wanted to tell you how sorry I am about Jenny. I know you were good friends.'

Maddy bowed her head but not before Rose had seen the sparkle of tears. Her outfit today was a little more subdued but still, Rose thought, bohemian, although for some reason she never quite succeeded in being more than a parody of herself. The thick black tights would be for warmth in the draughty shop but the deep purple skirt and the red sweater topped by a garish waistcoat were for effect. A large butterfly slide held back one side of her long, brittle blonde hair and what looked to Rose like fishing flies dangled from silver rods in her ears.

'I shall miss her more than anyone knows,' she said quietly then reached out a hand and pressed Rose's warm one. 'You're a very nice person, you know. Other people have hardly mentioned her to me.' Maddy was ashamed of her earlier antagonism towards Rose.

'Perhaps they didn't feel it was necessary. It's never easy in these situations.'

'Yes, perhaps you're right. I just wish I'd gone out after her that night like Nick . . .' She stopped abruptly and disappeared into the kitchen, leaving Rose wondering what she had been about to say. 'Like Nick said I should have?' 'Like Nick wished he had done?' Rose swallowed. 'Like Nick did?' It was beginning to seem as if everyone who had known Jenny was out in the streets that night.

She studied the room to the accompaniment of the clink of china and cutlery and the whine of the electric kettle as it came to the boil.

All the furniture was old-fashioned but not out of place with the building and although the windows were small the room was not as dark as it might have been because the curtains were hung well to the sides of the windows and did not cover the panes. On the floor was an old cord carpet, beige in colour. It was more practical than aesthetic but overlying it were a couple of bright rugs.

The ornaments and artefacts suggested no particular theme but were simply a random selection of pieces which Maddy liked. Rose had time to take this in before Maddy returned bearing a tray of coffee and a plate of cheese and biscuits. 'I couldn't be bothered to cut bread,' she admitted.

By the look of her face it seemed she had been crying. 'I'm seeing Stella this afternoon,' Rose said, trying to initiate some conversation. Something was seriously troubling Maddy. Guilt? Rose wondered, or guilty knowledge? Should she press her about Nick?

Maddy glanced towards the window, sticky with salt which had blown in with the wind and rain. 'You'll be lucky by the look of it. You know Stella won't get wet.' Her hands trembled as she picked up a cracker and a knife. 'Have you seen much of Nick lately?' She coloured, hating herself for asking the question.

'No. He's not ill, is he?' Rose frowned, unsure what Maddy was getting at.

'Oh, no, he's not ill.'

'Good. Anyway, I've been busy, I said I couldn't see him until Saturday.'

Maddy jumped to her feet, knocking her plate to the floor.

Rose was startled. Surely her harmless comment could not have caused such a reaction.

'So you're playing that little game, are you? Keeping him on a string, just like Jenny.'

Fighting the urge to get to her own feet and feel at less of a disadvantage, Rose tried to remain calm, tried to assess what turbulence was going on within the angry woman opposite her. 'No, I don't play games.'

'No, I don't play games.' Maddy mimicked her voice perfectly. 'Stringing him along, another bloody temperamental artist.'

'Maddy, I—'

'Oh, shut up. I know your sort. You've got a very high opinion of yourself. You use people, just like Jenny.'

So now we come to it, Rose thought. She equates Jenny with me because Nick was interested in us both. Rose was no longer sure if he *was* still interested in her, but this was irrelevant if Maddy believed otherwise. And Maddy was jealous, more than jealous. Was it the type of obsession which leads to insanity, even to murder?

Something was nagging at the back of her mind, some small action that Maddy had begun but not completed as they had entered the room. But something else struck her, too, her thoughts on Maddy having been at the mine. If she felt so strongly about Nick perhaps she had tried to entice Rose near the shaft hoping she would fall – or, worse, with the intention of pushing her.

Only seconds had passed. Maddy approached, shaking and white-faced. 'You deserve to die as well, you're just like that bitch.'

Rose tried to stand but it was too late. Strengthened by rage, Maddy grabbed at her throat, her strong potter's hands encircling it. Rose could not breathe. She knew that to panic would make matters worse. She had to fight back. Digging her heels into the base of the sofa she tried to force herself to her feet but only succeeded in sending the sofa backwards on its castors. She heard the sound of breaking porcelain. Maddy was on top of her, smothering her, but she had relinquished her grip. Her body was limp. 'Maddy,' Rose whispered. 'Oh, Maddy.'

'Oh, God, I'm so sorry,' she muttered before sobs shook her body and she started crying noisily into Rose's shoulder.

# CHAPTER SEVEN

'That's odd.' Stella replaced the receiver. It was unlike Rose not to ring if she couldn't make it. Stella shrugged, her glossy black hair fell forward. Well, it wasn't the end of the world if something more important had cropped up.

Having already arranged to take the afternoon off she decided to go out anyway. The rain seemed to have stopped at last. Downstairs in the gallery her assistant was talking to a potential customer. Stella stopped to chat, hoping that the presence of the artist herself might help clinch the sale. With a smile she said goodbye and stepped out into the narrow, winding street. To err on the safe side she was wearing a shiny black raincoat and carried a folding umbrella in her bag. She made her way down towards the harbour, taking pleasure in window-shopping, stopping to stare into one of the bakers' as she tried to decide if she was hungry. Stella believed people ought only to eat when they felt like it, not at regulated times. The smell of hot pasties was tempting but she knew she would not manage a whole one, not even a small one. Her stomach had been in knots for days.

Like Rose, she appreciated the individuality of the shops, all of which were small. There was none of the impersonality of the chain stores which offered the same goods in every town.

Stella almost tripped on the cobbles as she passed Maddy's place. She was still trying to work out how the girl had managed to be at all successful. Surely there was a limited market for the goods she sold, even the ones she made herself. Seeing a figure behind the counter she was about to wave when she realised it wasn't Maddy. She carried on until she came to the lifeboat station where she stood staring at the sand and the sea, wondering how it would be possible to bear it if she was ever to be parted from such beauty. A few minutes later she turned left, having decided to visit the Tate Gallery where there was a new exhibition. According to the newspapers the gallery had attracted literally millions of people to the area and she had to admit that the design of the building was terrific. Inside, if you stood to one side of the concave semicircular glass frontage, the bay was reflected in the glass opposite, as had been the architect's intention. Visitors took pictures of this but Stella doubted if they would show the full effect of the architecture.

Engrossed in the paintings of an artist unknown to her, she remained in the gallery for an hour and a half. As she left, she glanced back at the white edifice of the gallery which many people had so wrongly predicted would fail.

Crossing the road she stepped down on to the fine, white

sand. Her low heels sank into its softness and left tracks, the indentations of which were far larger than the size of her boots. Only when she reached the tide line were her footsteps reduced to normal dimensions as they stretched out behind her in the wet sand. A slight breeze ruffled the surface of the water but any surfers would have been disappointed that day. The frills of spray were only inches high. Despite the clarity of the air a vague headache lingered, the after-effects of last night, she thought. She and Daniel had sat down over a meal she had cooked with care and an expensive bottle of wine and talked out their differences. There was much that had needed to be said. Daniel had not previously understood the depth of the pain he had inflicted by his affair with Jenny. He had, he realised, been a fool to admit it, but it was over by then and he had wanted to tell Stella himself rather than have her hear it from another source. He and Jenny had been extremely careful, but that did not guarantee secrecy in a community where everyone knew each other.

Stella and Daniel had come to an agreement. They had sworn to try to put the affair behind them. But one thing was certain, it must not become known to the police. They would stick to the story that they had not been apart after the last guests had left the gallery. There was little chance that anyone could break their alibi. Stella had not passed a soul that night and there were certainly no people out on the cliffs. She smiled and dug the toe of her boot into the damp sand before turning and walking back up the beach.

We need to get away, she decided. Rarely did she and

Daniel leave Cornwall and then usually not together. One or other of them made infrequent visits to a city if they were showing their work but they had not had a holiday for many years. The trouble is, she thought, this county of mine makes you that way. It weaves its spell, making you feel that you can't leave the place. She knew many outsiders who had to return time and time again, most of whom had ambitions to retire to the area. The trouble was, what was there to go away for? No scenery could be better, no beaches more beautiful, no coastline more spectacular. And where else could you be so at peace? But that was just what was lacking at the moment, and Stella needed peace badly.

She turned to look back at the white specks of gulls drifting on air currents high in the sky. Then she walked on, the incoming tide following slowly on her heels as it swept up over the sand.

There was still no answer from Rose when she telephoned again, only her cheerful voice on the answering machine, but Stella felt certain that she wouldn't have forgotten their arrangement. Did she suspect something and prefer to keep out of the way? Rose Trevelyan was too observant for her own good, Stella thought. Perhaps she ought to find out just how much she knew. Telling Daniel she was going out in the car and she wasn't sure how long she'd be, she had to repeat herself. Working away at his sculpture, he hardly acknowledged her existence but Stella was not annoyed. She reacted in much the same way if she was disturbed. They would be all right, their marriage was back on solid ground and she intended it to remain that way.

\* \* \*

Jack and his team began to feel they were losing impetus. As the days passed they found that tongues were loosened, that people were not quite so reticent once they knew they were not the ones under suspicion. But instead of finding themselves nearer a solution, they merely discovered how many people had had cause to dislike Jennifer Manders. Not, they claimed, because she was unlikeable, far from it, it was agreed that she was good company, fun to be with, but her morals were a little questionable. And now it had been decided that Rose Trevelyan might hold the key. Her involvement appeared to be with not one, but both the corpses and, albeit inadvertently, she had led them to the first woman's burial place.

During that afternoon a detective sergeant tried Rose's number on six occasions but only got the answering machine. He did not leave a message. Inspector Pearce heard him grumbling to himself about people never being where you wanted them to be. Jack recognised the number on the display on the telephone. 'No luck?' he inquired, placing a file on the desk.

'Been at it since just before lunch.'

Jack frowned. 'Leave it with me.'

It was the sergeant's turn to frown. He had heard rumours that Jack and Mrs Trevelyan had once had a thing going; for all he knew they still did.

Jack glanced at the large round clock on the wall. Four-thirty and daylight had long faded. Returning to his office he tried the number himself with no result. Then he left the building, shrugging his arms into his coat as he did so. His mind turned to the statement Alec Manders had made. What sort of a father was he to have virtually ignored Jenny in the years when it mattered, to have allowed his own mother, rather than the girl's, so much say? Jack had wondered about that. Renata Manders had disappeared, that much was common knowledge, and with another man. But Jack's suspicions had proved groundless when he had asked to see the marriage certificate and the divorce papers.

It had crossed his mind that the woman in the shaft might have been Renata. If she and Manders had not been married but had only lived as man and wife, there would have been no need for Manders to produce a decree absolute in order to marry Angela. If he had lied it might have been because Renata had never left the area and he had used the non-existent divorce which was supposed to have taken place six years later as an alibi. Jack was disappointed when he was shown the documentary evidence which proved his theory wrong.

Of Jennifer he had learnt little. It was as if her father had hardly known her. Despite the fact that they lived so close to one another they rarely came into contact. Jenny's friends had borne this out. Why, Jack had wanted to know, had Jenny not gone to her father when her financial situation had reduced her to living in a squat? Alec said he did not know.

And as for the mystery woman, there seemed, for the moment, nowhere else to turn. It was time to concentrate on the weeks leading up to Jenny's death and probe a little more deeply into the alibis of those who had known her. It made Jack feel sick. Rose was without an alibi and she had now admitted that she had known Jenny was with Nick when he telephoned. There was no one to say she had not got back into the car and driven over to St Ives to wait for her to leave.

Traffic was building up. He cursed at the slow-moving queue at the roundabout by Tesco's. When he finally reached Rose's house he saw at once that she wasn't at home. There was no car in the drive and no lights shining from the windows. A sixth sense told him that she would not let matters rest, that she would end up in danger. He ought not to have ignored her for so long. If he had made more effort she would have confided in him or at least alerted him to her plans. Laura might know, he thought, and used his mobile phone to contact her rather than waste time by driving to her house.

'I'm sure she said she was taking a day off and going to St Ives. Jack, is she in trouble?'

'I don't know.' He didn't want to cause alarm. 'Do you know exactly where she was going?'

Jack's stomach muscles knotted. Knowing Rose she would start asking questions, would antagonise people and possibly place herself in danger. He had to find her. It was not like her to be out all day unless she was working, but as it was dark that was now an impossibility. 'Thanks, Laura.' He started the engine and headed towards St Ives. But which of them to approach first?

The interior lights of Stella's gallery were off and the sign on the door said 'Closed' but a spotlight illuminated a single large painting in the corner of the window. He rang the bell and waited. A man appeared in the dimness and unlocked the door. Ever observant, Jack did not miss the flinch as Daniel Wright's eyes registered instant recognition.

'Come in, please.'

Jack followed him up the spiral staircase. By the window, staring out into the darkness, was Stella, her tall willowy figure dressed in black, relieved only by a scarlet and gold scarf at her neck. Her hair gleamed and from behind she might have been oriental.

'Ms Jackson?' He hated the appellation but in this case could not think of a more appropriate one. 'I have to tell you that I'm here unofficially so you have every right to refuse to answer my questions. I'm trying to find Rose Trevelyan and I wondered if you had any idea where she might be.'

'How odd. I've been trying to get hold of her myself.' Stella walked across the polished boards of the floor and sat down, her posture as elegant as a model's. 'You see, she was supposed to come here this afternoon. We'd arranged to meet at two and go out somewhere.' She lifted her hands in a helpless gesture. 'I thought she'd changed her mind although I was very surprised she didn't ring me to say so. When she didn't arrive by three I tried ringing her and again twice since but I only get her answering machine. About teatime I drove over to her house but there was no one there. Do you suppose something's happened to her?'

Does she mean anything by that? Jack asked himself. At least this confirmed what Laura had told him, Rose had been making for St Ives. Then where the hell is she? he thought. There had been no road traffic accidents that day, at least none that warranted police attention, so that ruled out one possibility. Besides, Rose had her mobile phone. He was sure he knew Rose better than Stella Jackson did and he would have sworn that she would have let Stella know if she had decided not to come. 'So you don't have any idea where she might have gone instead?'

'No. I suppose you could try Nick Pascoe. Other than that I can't help. I don't know her friends in Newlyn.'

Jack's jaw tightened at the mention of Nick's name. What if it was that simple, that Rose was there with him now, and he barged in to find them in a compromising situation? He did not think he could cope with that. But he must find Rose, he must know that she was safe. It was Daniel who showed him out, now smiling and chatting easily, his relief at not being questioned all too obvious. Jack decided to think about that later. Never again would he accuse Rose of meddling. Right now he was doing precisely that himself.

In order to regain his professional objectivity he drove around aimlessly for a few minutes, preparing himself for what he dreaded discovering at Pascoe's place. Seconds after he passed the car-park he stopped dangerously quickly, relieved that there was no car behind him. Had he seen right? Finding a place to turn he went back. Rose's car was parked neatly in an allocated space. The doors, when he got out to check them, were locked. Then she is with Nick, he thought. Controlling his anger at the idea of them together and her lack of consideration for Stella, he drove to Nick's small stone house. The curtains were open and as he approached the front door Jack saw a man in shirtsleeves moving about the room. He knocked and waited. Pascoe opened the door. He was unshaven and looked a mess and he rubbed his eyes as he spoke. His breath smelt of alcohol, but not offensively so. A cigarette trailed smoke in an ashtray. 'Come in. Excuse the state of the place.'

'Are you all right, Mr Pascoe?' The man seemed exhausted, although it might be the physical effects of fear.

'Yes and no. Nothing serious. Insomnia, the bane of my life. I almost resorted to that—' he indicated a bottle of gin – '*but* decided against it after two glasses. It won't solve anything and I'll only feel worse in the morning.'

'Mr Pascoe, I'm trying to locate Rose Trevelyan. Have you any idea where she might be?'

'No.' He sounded genuinely surprised. 'I haven't seen her all week. She said she couldn't see me until Saturday.'

Jack's face was expressionless. He was pleased to hear that but also disappointed that she intended seeing Nick again.

'Have you tried Stella? She goes there sometimes.'

'Yes.'

Nick shrugged. 'In that case I can't help you. I'm sorry, can I offer you something? Coffee or a drink if that's allowed?'

'No. I'm fine, thanks.' Jack turned to leave. 'If she does get in touch, will you let me know?' He handed Nick a card.

'Of course. Oh, God, you don't think anything's happened to *her* now, do you?'

'I hope not, Mr Pascoe. I sincerely hope not.' Twice in less than half an hour he had been asked that question. Did these people know something? Were they all in it together?

Jack had been about to leave. He paused and turned. 'Do you often have trouble sleeping?'

'Yes. On and off over the years.'

'How do you overcome it?'

Nick shrugged. 'I don't. I refuse to resort to drugs, I tend to work or read or walk.'

'And on the night Jennifer Manders died?'

'I've already told you. She came here and we talked, then she left. I can't tell you any more than that.' Nick spoke too quickly and Jack could hear the rising panic in his voice. 'Oh, Christ!' He sank into a chair, knowing it was useless to dissemble further, his head in his hands. Jack waited. 'I should've told you before. I don't know why I didn't. I did go out that night. About twenty minutes after Jenny left. I spoke to Maddy and hearing how upset Jenny was I thought I ought to look for her. Once, I thought I saw her in the distance. I called out but whoever it was too far away to hear. Then I lost sight of her. That was it.'

'Mr Pascoe, you do realise the seriousness of what you've told me? You can be charged with withholding evidence. May I use your telephone?'

Nick nodded, knowing what must happen next.

Jack requested a car to come and take Nick to Camborne where he would be asked to revise his statement. Pascoe had been drinking and Jack, who could have driven him, was more intent upon finding Rose. 'You'll be here when the car comes?'

'I won't be running away.' He laughed cynically. 'Where would I go?'

If her car's still here, Jack thought whilst at the same

time hoping Pascoe could be trusted, she can't be far away, but where else was there to look? He left his own car parked near Pascoe's house and walked down towards West Pier then along The Wharf, stopping to gaze at the water which now filled the harbour and which was perfectly calm and still. Boats swayed imperceptibly on their moorings as the tide began to ebb. Almost opposite him, at the end of Smeaton's Pier, was the lighthouse.

I'll walk as far as that, he decided, and then I'll know what to do next. For the moment his next step was unclear.

A few minutes later he stopped, unable to believe what he was seeing. Walking towards him, her hair loose and blowing gently around her shoulders, was a small figure in a skirt and top, raincoat open and flapping in time with her footsteps. 'Rose?' he whispered. Then 'Rose!' he shouted.

Rose stood still and looked up, squinting into the darkness. Jack walked swiftly towards her. 'My God,' he said breathlessly. 'Are you all right?'

'Oh, I think so. A little shaken, but not hurt. And also extremely puzzled.'

'About what?'

She shook her head.

'Can I buy you a drink? Have you eaten?'

'No. No, I haven't.' She had difficulty in remembering,

Controlling an impulse to grab her hand Jack walked beside her, shortening his stride so as not to hurry her. They went into a small pub in Fore Street and joined the other customers. The beams were low and Jack had to duck beneath them. They stood at the curved bar in the over-warm room.

'You're pale,' he said when he had got their drinks. 'Why don't we sit down?'

Rose knew he preferred to stand but her legs felt weak so she complied.

'I think you'd better tell me what's going on, Rose.'

'I went to see Maddy Duke. I had arranged to see Stella but I was early so I thought I'd take the opportunity to buy Barry's present.' Jack flinched. Last year he had been given one. 'She invited me upstairs once the shop was closed for lunch. I wanted to talk to her, you see, because I remembered some remarks she made at Stella's that night. Remarks to Jenny about me and Nick. I had an inkling then that she fancied him herself. It made me wonder whether she was jealous and had somehow rigged those screams at the mine.'

'But what would she gain from that?'

Rose sniffed. 'No idea. Perhaps she thought I'd walk towards the sound and fall down the shaft or maybe she simply intended to scare me to put me off painting. Stella once said that Maddy was jealous of anyone with talent. I can't say I'd noticed, but Stella knows her better. Anyway, before we got a chance to talk she attacked me.'

'What?'

Rose nodded and ran a tired hand across her forehead. 'At one point I thought she was going to kill me.'

'My God.'

'I'd ruined her plans, you see. With Jenny out of the way she thought she had a chance with Nick.'

'I see.'

'I don't think you do, Jack. I managed to explain that

there was nothing between us. At first I thought that there might be. I was attracted to him but it didn't take long to discover that apart from the fact that he isn't really looking for a relationship it wouldn't have worked.'

'Why not? If that's not too personal a question.'

Rose turned to look at him. There was a spot of colour on each of Jack's cheekbones and he appeared momentarily vulnerable. 'He would have been too demanding. He's talented but he's very moody and he would have expected me to pander to his moods. And that's not for me, Jack.'

'As I well know.'

'I intend telling him at the weekend, face to face.'

As you did with me, Jack thought, then grinned. Poor bastard, he didn't know what he was in for.

They were quiet for a few minutes, each thinking about what they had shared, Jack hoping it could be rekindled, Rose glad that she still had his friendship. 'That can't be all.' His tone was brisk now. 'There must have been more to make her behave in such a way.'

'There was. When she'd calmed down enough to speak coherently she burst into tears and couldn't stop apologising. I felt so sorry for her, she was so pathetic and forlorn. I can't understand how women can get that way about a man who has no interest in them. She'd been to see Nick this morning and he'd turned her away, just as he had Jenny.

'She'd closed for lunch but after that dramatic scene I thought it better if Sally, that's the girl who helps her out, came in and took over. She was surprised, for some reason. Anyway, Maddy begged me to stay; she really was in an

164

awful state. We went through the same thing all over again: the tears and apologies. I realised it wasn't safe to leave her on her own. By then I'd forgotten about Stella and when I did remember it didn't seem right ringing from there.

'When she was less emotional she was terribly embarrassed by what she had done and I could see that she wanted to talk. She admitted how lonely she was and how hard she'd tried to be one of the crowd. Oh, Jack, she really is a mess. She told me she had a child when she was young and her parents made her have it adopted.'

'Made her?'

'Yes. It's a complicated story, but they did. For that, she's never forgiven them or herself. What a way to live, wrapped up in a guilt you can't share or rid yourself of. Something else was interesting, too.' Rose rested her chin on her knuckles, her elbows on the table in front of her. 'I didn't believe her at first but when I thought about it I saw it was possible and that, without my noticing it, the same thing might have been happening to me. She said Stella's always putting her down.'

'How do you mean?'

'It's difficult to explain but it's as if the compliments Stella pays are deliberately back-handed. For instance, in my case she says my painting is good but I've still got a lot of hard work to do, and maybe one day I'll make it, that sort of thing. In Maddy's case she makes jibes about how surprising it is that so many people want to buy the sort of things she makes for "her little shop" as she puts it. And then she'll make a point of saying not everyone can be a great artist, as if this is supposed to cheer us both up.'

'Rose, she might have killed Jenny because she wanted Nick.'

'I'm sure she didn't. She admitted there were times she could've strangled her, especially when she told Maddy that she was going to try to get Nick back. And then she said . . .'

'Rose?'

Rose sighed with resignation. 'Then she said she'd seen Nick that night after she'd spoken to him on the phone.'

'I know.'

'What?'

'He told me. He's at Camborne now.' I hope, he added silently.

Rose was relieved. She knew it was her duty to inform Jack but it was better that Nick had done so himself. Here goes, she thought. 'There's something else.' She couldn't meet his eyes. These were her friends. 'Daniel Wright once told me that Stella always goes for a long walk after an opening night. Not that I'm saying she did,' Rose added hastily, glancing at his stern expression. 'It could've been an exception.'

The whole bloody lot of them seem to have been wandering around the streets of St Ives, Jack thought gloomily. So it's back to square one again. 'Is there anything else you feel I should know?'

Rose recognised the sarcasm but chose to ignore it. 'Well, yes, actually.' That'll teach you, she thought, gaining a brief satisfaction from the tightening of his jaw. 'Mind you, I don't know if it's relevant. Maddy has a collection of tapes. Ones she's made herself of her friends' voices.'

'What on earth for?'

166

Rose didn't answer for a few seconds. She was recalling the action which Maddy had curtailed, one which she now knew would have led to her own voice being recorded. The recorder was well hidden, Maddy only had to bend to flick a switch. Perhaps she sensed how the conversation would go and had thought better of it. 'She'll make a good actress, she got my voice off to perfection.'

'Rose, what're you talking about? What recordings?'

'To help her with her acting. Oh, don't you know?'

'No. Tell me.' Jack leant back and folded his arms. Rose Trevelyan was a totally infuriating woman at times.

'Well, she joined the amateur dramatic company some months ago but she couldn't get parts because she, to use her own words, always came out sounding like Maddy Duke. She taped other voices and practised copying them.'

'And?'

'And she's got a part in the Christmas pantomime.'

Jack took a sip of his drink. His arm brushed against Rose's as he replaced his glass. He felt weak. 'Are you sure that's the only purpose of the tapes?' Jack could think of others, such as blackmail or using the recordings of her friends, edited, to cause who knew what mischief by way of a telephone.

'Mm. I think so. Except, and this is going to sound daft, it crossed my mind that she thinks she might feel more part of things if she had a touch of a Cornish accent.'

Jack shook his head in disbelief. Women's minds were often incomprehensible to him. He moved in his seat. Rose's flowery perfume was disturbing him now. However, Maddy Duke sounded like a suitable case for treatment: insanely jealous of everyone, making peculiar tapes, attacking a so-called friend and yearning for a long-lost baby. He sighed. Another suspect back on the list. 'What time did you leave her?'

'About an hour before I met you. Maddy went back down to the shop to relieve Sally. She was fine by then. I needed some air. It'd been a damn long afternoon. Jack, what's bothering you?'

'You are. Be careful, Rose. Think how much you know already. Whoever killed Jenny might not like it. And a couple of my colleagues are wondering why you're taking such an interest.'

'Oh, you mean they think I'm trying to cover my tracks?'

'There's no need for sarcasm, Rose. Most people prefer to distance themselves from crime of any sort.'

'But I'm not most people, am I, Jack, or you wouldn't be here now.'

Her comment hurt. 'Look, have you thought that someone may have been trying to implicate you rather than scare you?'

'How come?' This had not occurred to her.

'You've lived here long enough to have been a contemporary of the woman in the shaft. Guilt has strange ways of manifesting itself.'

'Including auditory hallucinations?'

'Yes. And returning to the scene of the crime. After that, you become involved with a man who's given his girlfriend, younger girlfriend, the boot and then you learn she wants him back. It wouldn't take a genius to set you up for both things.'

'But you don't even know who the first woman was.'

'No. But you might.'

Rose was very worried. Who would want to do that to her, and why? She looked down. Jack's hand was resting on her knee but it was a fraternal gesture.

'Jennifer Manders didn't lack for companions with whom to share pillow talk. There could be other men we don't know about, so don't think we've stopped looking.'

Rose knew she ought to voice her suspicions. Why hold back now? 'It's possible Jenny had an affair with Daniel Wright.'

'How do you know?' he asked quietly.

'I don't. It was just an impression I got. Oh, Jack, I really hate all this. These people are my friends.' She was near to tears.

'One other thing. I think Stella's jealous of your talent.'

'Stella? Don't be ridiculous.' But perhaps it was not as ridiculous as it sounded. There were the put-downs which Rose, who was unaware of the strength of her own self-possession, had not noticed until Maddy had pointed them out, and the advice not to go to a certain gallery owner because he charged an extortionate commission. Later Rose had found this to be untrue but assumed Stella had been mistaken. The idea of her friends being guilty was repugnant. She liked them, despite their various flaws, or maybe because of them. She recalled part of a conversation with Doreen Clarke who had telephoned for a chat recently. Penzance, Newlyn and Hayle were Doreen's known territories; she had, in her own words, no truck with St Ives people. 'Different breed, they,' she had remarked enigmatically. Rose smiled inwardly. To Doreen, anyone not from her own locality might as well have come from a different planet.

'How's Jenny's father taken it?'

Jack, too, had been deep in thought. He had a feeling that Rose's friends, no matter how stringently questioned, would all stick together. 'It's hard to say. I don't think he had much time for her.'

'I got that impression too.'

Jack closed his eyes. What now? he thought. What is she going to surprise me with this time? 'You've spoken to him?'

'I'd met him briefly a month or so ago. I was over in St Ives and he and Jenny had just bumped into each other. She introduced me. I thought, as I'd known her, the least I could now do was to tell her father how sorry I was. I couldn't have done that once, Jack. After David died so many people avoided me. They didn't know what to do or say, they were afraid they'd make things worse. It doesn't, though. However clumsy or lacking in tact people are, it's still a comfort to know they care.' He looks exhausted, Rose realised. Jack's clothes were creased and the lines which gave his face character were amplified with tiredness and frustration.

'I'm sorry, Rose. I didn't think of it that way.'

'You thought, as Barry would say, I was interfering?' She took a sip of her wine. 'I suppose in a way I was. You see, I wondered whether the skeleton you found was Jenny's mother.'

Jack grinned. He immediately looked years younger. 'So did I.'

'And?'

He shook his head. 'I've discussed far too much with you already, Mrs Trevelyan. My major suspect, too. Hey, what're you thinking about now?'

Rose's brow had creased in a frown. 'Something Maddy said. I can't remember exactly what it was, but I'm sure she mentioned that Jenny said if Nick didn't take her back she'd go and live with her father again. But she didn't, did she? She ended up living rough. Still, I suppose if they didn't get on it wouldn't have worked. To be honest, the man gave me the creeps. I wonder if Renata'll go to the funeral.'

'There won't be any funeral, at least not for a while. The inquest hasn't even been opened yet. Anyway, what made you say that?'

'Well . . .' Rose began, feeling herself blushing because she hadn't asked Alec Manders whether his ex-wife would be coming down out of mere politeness. She had asked because she was as curious as everyone else was to know the identity of the first body and, like Jack, she had thought it might be Renata. 'He was evasive. I got the impression she might not even know her daughter was dead.'

'He told us he'd written to her.' Jack left it at that. He should not be discussing this with Rose but by giving her an answer he hoped to deter her from getting in deeper. Other officers were seeking the veracity of Manders' comment. 'Are you up to driving?'

'Yes, I'm fine, thanks.'

'Then I'll walk you to your car. And I want you to go straight home and stay there.'

Rose looked up at him and grinned. 'Yes, Inspector. Anything you say, sir.'

With a warm feeling of satisfaction Jack watched her drive away. They had parted on more amicable terms than on many recent occasions. But he knew Rose better than to read too much into that.

# CHAPTER EIGHT

Because of the two consecutive inquiries, extra men had been drafted in from Charles Cross police station in Plymouth. Jack Pearce always felt a nagging resentment when this happened although he knew it was necessary.

He had come to some conclusions but was, for the moment, keeping them to himself. One thing he would like to do might or might not be approved. It would be costly and would take time but he thought it would probably be necessary in the end. For the moment the old method, the question and answer system, would suffice. And there was one question he really wanted an answer to.

Why, if the woman in the mine had fallen or been pushed, had she crawled further into the shaft instead of staying where she could see daylight above and where, if she called for help, she had the faintest chance of being heard? As in Jenny's case, it had to be that she had been killed first then her body taken down there and hidden. Colleagues agreed with him when they had discussed the similarities here. The method was the same in both cases. Forensics could not be certain and would only go as far as to say that it was possible, but they suspected the damage to the skull was in excess of what might be expected from such a fall. Both women hit over the head, then the bodies hidden in such a manner that if they were discovered their deaths might seem accidental. The same person? How neat that would be. Scene-of-crime officers had been of little use in Jenny's case. The evidence would be where she was killed, not on the edge of the sea. The laborious forensic task of examining cars and other forms of transport was about to begin. Everyone who had known Jenny was being reinterviewed. Someone had moved the body, but how and from where? Boat owners of every description were being questioned. Information obtained from the coastguards regarding tides and currents suggested she had been taken some distance out to sea and thrown overboard. Had Jennifer Manders fallen from the cliffs anywhere along the stretch where she was found her body would have been washed up farther down the coast.

Jack sat at his desk, staring unseeingly at the work awaiting his attention. Not a fisherman or experienced seaman, he told himself. Whoever had tried to make it seem as if she had fallen and drowned had made a mistake.

The necessary paperwork to bring in the suspects' cars for examination, had they been unwilling to cooperate, had been issued. Jack was grateful that the advances in technology meant that, no matter how thoroughly a vehicle may have been cleaned, traces of blood and fibres would still be detectable. He realised he had been sitting there for over half an hour and hadn't achieved a thing.

Nick Pascoe had amended his statement the previous evening. He did not think anyone had seen him returning home after only fifteen minutes when he failed to catch up with the woman he believed was Jenny. Jack frowned. But Maddy Duke had said she had remained in her seat in the window until almost one a.m. It was where she always sat as she worked. Surely she would have noticed him? Any movement at that time of night in the quiet streets would have been noticeable even if his footsteps hadn't echoed in the night air. He would ask her about it when he questioned her again later that day.

By the time he left for home Jack's handsome face was drawn with fatigue. The problem here was not too many alibis but a complete lack of them. Rose, like everyone else, was still under suspicion.

By the weekend they had reached a hiatus. The frenzy of the initial inquiry was over, the repetitive slogging was to come. It would have been nice to talk to Rose, to discover her views, but for the moment he must avoid her. Maddy Duke had only repeated that she had not seen Pascoe return. It was beginning to look as if Jack's feelings about him were correct. However, for the moment, they did not have enough evidence to arrest him. Tests were being done on his car. Jack was banking on the results of these to back up his theory. As for the unknown woman, every division in the country now had the details and would be going back through their records of missing persons.

Dressing with care on Saturday morning Rose thought about what she had learnt from her own solicitor whom she had telephoned the day before. Apart from the purchase of the house and David's probate she had had little need of Charles Kingsman's services over the years although, having known David long before he did Rose, he seemed to feel obliged to keep an eye on his widow and got in touch every couple of months or so. Not learnt, Rose realised, I'd already worked it out. I needed it confirmed. She sprayed perfume on her neck and wrists and wondered how she could let Nick know, as tactfully as possible, that friendship was as much as she wanted from him. Flicking back her hair she grinned at herself in the mirror. My tact may be wasted if he's not interested anyway, she thought.

Nick was punctual and told her at once how lovely she looked, although she was not terribly flattered by the look of surprise on his face as he took in her appearance. She didn't always look a mess. 'Thanks,' she said, looking down at the plain pale blue dress she had bought when away on a business trip with Barry. It had been one of her better buys. She picked up her raincoat. It wasn't raining but it was the only outer garment which went with the dress.

'New car?' Rose asked, as he opened the door for her.

'No. Hired.' He paused. 'The police still have mine.'

'Oh.' There was little she could say. Nick was obviously still very much a suspect. She wished she hadn't asked and she tried to put from her mind the thought that she was possibly sitting next to Jenny's killer. They drove the rest of the way in way silence.

'Anywhere in particular you want to go?' Nick asked as they joined the throngs of shoppers.

'Not really. Shall we just stroll around and try not to get ourselves injured in the crush?' The pavements were overflowing.

They window-shopped for almost an hour, mooching around the alleyways and the markets, and stopping to admire the cathedral, which was built smack in the centre and towered overhead between the low-storey buildings. By twelve-thirty they were still empty-handed and decided they might as well eat.

There was a wine bar nearby and they were early enough to get a decent table before the real rush began. It was typical of its kind: bare floorboards, tables with wrought-iron legs and marble tops and the cutlery presented in a rolled paper serviette. But the menu was interesting and the list of wines extensive. 'You choose,' Nick said, referring to the wine. 'You'll have to drink most of it.'

More people came in as they waited for their food. Rose ordered the Greek salad because she preferred to eat her main meal in the evening; Nick went for the more substantial pork and apricot stew with French bread.

'It's gone very quiet,' Nick commented when they had taken their first few mouthfuls.

Rose, a piece of pitta bread halfway to her mouth, looked around at the other chatting customers. 'What has?'

'The investigation.'

'I'd hardly say that. Jack said they're speaking to everyone again.'

'Yes.' He stared at something beyond Rose's shoulder because he was embarrassed to look at her. 'But we've all been to Camborne now and nothing's happened. No arrest, I mean.'

Rose wondered whether he was fishing, whether he believed because of her friendship with Inspector Pearce she would be privy to certain information. 'They're still testing the vehicles. I don't get mine back until tomorrow.' But Nick's, she realised, had been the first to be taken. Was that relevant? How she would have loved to know what went on in those interviews. Had Jack questioned Daniel about his relationship with Jenny? Had Maddy been more forthcoming after the catharsis of her outburst? And did the confirmation from Charles Kingsman mean what she thought it might mean? For the moment she must think about Nick and the appropriate words to explain how she felt about him.

'There's that other woman, too. I gather they still don't know who she is.'

The turn in the conversation had dampened Rose's mood and the carols playing in the background seemed to mock them. It was time to change the subject and talk of something more cheerful. Nick's work, she decided, would be a starting place.

'I haven't done much, lately, what with not sleeping and

the miserable weather. No, to be honest, I just haven't felt like it. What about you?'

'Plodding along.' Rose speared an olive.

'I still find that business out at the mine baffling. Haven't the police come up with anything on that?'

'I think they've got more important problems on their mind.' This was not true. She knew that Jack believed there was a definite connection with what she had heard and what they had found. Rose was disappointed. As hard as she had tried to change the subject Nick kept reverting to it. The day was not turning out the way she had anticipated, and they finished the meal in another uncomfortable silence. Rose was annoyed because Nick could have made more of an effort. She wondered why she had bothered to come and why he had bothered to ask her, and, more to the point, why she had not told him how their relationship stood.

Deciding against coffee, Rose poured the last of the wine and lit a cigarette.

'I didn't know you smoked.'

Nick's tone was disapproving which infuriated Rose further. There were ashtrays on every table, it was not as if she was acting illegally. 'Well, I do. Not often, and not many, but I do enjoy one after a meal. I'll drink this then we'll go.' She indicated the inch or two of wine in her glass.

'I'm sorry, Rose, I really don't know what's got into me. Everything I say comes out wrong. I wasn't criticising.'

You were, Rose thought but did not say. Instead she

smiled. 'It was a nice meal. Thank you.' He had insisted beforehand that he paid.

The streets seemed even busier as they left the wine bar. Between the buildings the sky was grey, not the greyness which promised rain but that of the half-light of an afternoon in late December. 'It's Stella's party tomorrow. Are you going?'

'She's invited me,' Nick replied.

My God, Rose thought, hastening her footsteps. What's wrong with a simple yes or no? He really is in a mood. 'Nick, is something bothering you?'

'No. Just the culmination of too many nights without proper sleep.'

'Shall we go back now? There's nothing I need to buy.'

'If you like.'

'I do like.' Several people stopped. Rose was unaware how loudly she had spoken but she found Nick's diffidence extremely infuriating.

The journey back was as silent as the one coming and Rose was angry. There was nothing wrong with not speaking if it was a companionable silence, as she often experienced with Barry and Laura and even Jack. This was downright moodiness. Rose was about to tell Nick to drop her in St Ives to save himself the extra miles when he rested a hand on her thigh and gave it a quick squeeze. 'I've behaved dreadfully. Forgive me. I just didn't realise how much Jenny's death had upset me. It's taken a while to sink in. I keep thinking I'll see her around the next corner.'

Now it was Rose who felt ashamed. How could she have

not realised what he must be going through? They had lived together for over three years and it was less than a week since Jenny's body had been found. The man was grieving and she had expected him to entertain her. On top of that he probably felt guilty for having sent her away that night. 'It's hard, isn't it? Look, let's pretend today never happened and take it from there.'

'You're rather special, Rose Trevelyan. Don't let anyone ever tell you otherwise.'

With the change of mood Rose agreed to go back to Nick's house where, he said, she could listen to some decent music and drink more wine if she wanted because she wasn't driving. 'I'll abstain if you need a lift home. If you want to stay there's a spare room.'

Tactfully put, she thought. It leaves every option open. But in the end she drank only one glass of Chablis.

Nick opened the door and switched on the fire, knowing that most people felt the cold more than himself. Having settled Rose into the corner of the settee he went to get the wine from the fridge. Rose leant back and listened to the swelling music of Beethoven. 'Thanks.' She took her glass which was misted with condensation and sipped the icy contents. 'Delicious, it's one of my favourites.' Cynically she wondered if this was the classic seduction scene; if so, Nick was about to be disappointed. And the flickering flames were from a coal-effect electric fire rather than a real one. She placed the wine on the small table beside her from which Nick had removed a pile of papers. As she moved back something firm nudged her hip. She reached down and pulled a hard-backed book from between the side of the settee and the cushion. It was a novel – a new one, only recently published. She had read the reviews. Nick had told her he didn't read novels. Always curious she opened it to read the blurb but before she could do so her eyes were drawn to the inscription. 'To Jenny, a gift to thank you for last weekend.' Rose's face felt hot and she closed the book quickly but not before Nick had seen her.

'I can explain,' he said.

'There's no need. It's none of my business.' But he looked so shifty that Rose wanted to hear that explanation.

Nick was on his feet. He slid one hand into the back pocket of his jeans and turned away, unable to look at her. His other hand raked through his hair.

I like the way his hair lies across his collar, Rose thought, surprised at her objectivity, because she now knew for certain that what little had existed between them before no longer did.

'She came here a few times. After she'd left, that is.'

'Nick, I'd rather not hear this.'

'There was nothing in it.' He smiled. 'She cooked me a meal. To make up for all those other times she didn't, I expect.'

'Nick, I'd like to go now. There's no need for you to drive me, I'll make my own way home.' He's lying, she thought. He's looking me straight in the eye and lying to me. It was never really over between them. Not for one moment could she imagine Jenny turning up just to cook a meal because she had been remiss in this regard before. And if he had still been seeing her did that make him more of a suspect or less?

'Please, don't go. I thought we were getting on so well.'

'I must. I have things to do.' She picked up her raincoat, put it on then grabbed her handbag decisively. 'Thanks again for the lunch.'

'Rose?'

'Bye, Nick.' She tried to smile but her face felt stiff.

Hurrying down the road she knew she was lucky it was still early, not much after three. There would be a choice of a train or a bus. No one stood at any of the stops she passed so she continued down into the main part of St Ives and up the hill towards the Malakof where the buses waited and which was adjacent to the railway station. The track was single-line, and the same train chugged back and forth. In the distance she saw it snake around the edge of the bay towards her. At least something was in her favour. She walked down the slope to the car-park and across it to the platform.

When the train arrived she got on and sat down, pressing her hot face against the window. It misted with her breath. Only a couple of other passengers joined her and soon they were rattling over the track. In less than twenty minutes she was back in Penzance.

They had walked a fair distance that morning but Rose needed air. She started making her way along by the harbour and on to the Promenade then decided to detour, to walk up into the town centre and see Barry. She longed for the honest solidity of him but recognised that she was using him. On the other hand, over the years he had tried to convince her that that was what friends were for, they were the people to whom you turned when you needed a sympathetic ear. Rose needed one then.

Barry was delighted to see her although he expressed concern for her appearance. 'You look a bit peaky, woman,' he said.

Rose smiled reassuringly. 'I'm fine. Anyway, I decided, as it's Saturday, I'm going to let you buy me a drink.'

'How very kind of you.' Barry thumbed his glasses back into place. There were red indentations on either side of his nose.

Rose waited the forty-odd minutes until he closed the shop and cashed up the till. Outside he locked the door, pushed it to check it was safe, then, after half a dozen paces, turned back to check again. Rose shook her head. He always did it and had once driven from her place in the middle of the evening to double-check because he couldn't remember having turned the key in the Chubb lock beneath the Yale.

Together they walked up to the London Inn in Causewayhead. Ensconced in the back bar, Rose downed a glass of wine quickly. Her face burned. It was dark outside but some shops were still open. Through the frosted glass window they saw shapes walking past. 'I think I'm beginning to feel quite festive,' Rose said.

Barry studied her face. 'I don't think festive's the right word, Rosie. Do you want me to get you a taxi?'

'No.' Suddenly she was serious. 'I don't want to go home just yet.' Never in all the years she had lived in the house had she felt that way. It held nothing but happy memories.

Barry stroked her cheek. It was an avuncular gesture. 'What is it, Rose?'

'For one thing I'm a suspect. I had to go back and answer the same questions all over again. Jack thinks I killed Jenny and that other woman.'

'He thinks no such thing, and you know it. That's not what's really bothering you.'

'No. You're right. I don't know what's got into me. And it hurts to know my friends are under suspicion. I feel I ought to be able to tell if any one of them killed Jenny.'

'Why should you when the police can't?'

'I know. It's illogical. And there's Nick.'

'Ah. Yes. Nick.' Barry studied the contents of his glass and uncharitably wished he was the guilty party.

'It's over, you see. Well, not that much was going on anyway. I won't be seeing him again.'

Barry's spontaneous boyish grin left Rose in no doubt how he felt about that piece of news. 'Can I get you another drink?' She stood with her own glass in her hand.

Barry noticed the blue dress, the one she had bought to wear out to dinner in London with him. With her flushed face she looked lovely. 'One more then you're going home. Order a taxi while you're at the bar.'

The taxi turned up promptly twenty minutes later. Arriving home she heard the telephone ringing as she unlocked the kitchen door and reached it seconds before the answering machine cut in.

'It's me. Nick. I've tried several times but I didn't want

to leave a message. I behaved disgracefully today. I hope you can forgive me. About Jenny, it was—'

'Please, Nick. I don't want to hear any more about Jenny.'

'Can I see you tomorrow?'

'No.'

'But you'll still come to Stella's?'

'There's no reason for me not to.' I can be as evasive as you, she thought.

'Good. Until then.'

'Nick, I'd rather you didn't ring me any more. I don't need complications in my life at the moment. Goodbye.' Rose replaced the receiver before he had a chance to argue.

In the morning Rose sat at the kitchen table sipping coffee and nibbling at a piece of toast. It was 23rd December, the day of Stella's party. The coffee tasted strange and it hurt to swallow. By mid-morning her head was thumping and she felt sore all over. Her limbs felt heavy and it was an effort to stand as she dialled Stella's number to make her apologies. She was in no state to attend a party. Having swallowed two aspirins and filled a jug with fruit juice, Rose took herself to bed with a hot water bottle. For most of that day and long into the night she sweated out a dose of flu, not caring whether Nick thought it was an excuse to avoid him.

Too weak to do more than sit and read she spent a miserable Christmas Eve. Laura rang and offered to come over and cheer her up but Rose said she preferred to be on her own and the last thing Laura needed was to catch her germs when her whole family was there.

Luckily the bug was short-lived and she awoke on Christmas morning feeling better. After a leisurely breakfast, accompanied by a giant crossword she had saved for the occasion, she made a couple of telephone calls. Barry was delighted with his penholder and Laura with her earrings. 'It sounds like pandemonium,' Rose commented. In the background she could hear laughter and male voices and the high-pitched ones of excited children.

'It is. Must go, someone's calling me. Thanks, Rose. Happy Christmas,' Laura said.

At midday she uncorked a bottle of champagne and, an hour later, ate a lunch of smoked salmon and a ready-cooked chicken with salad. It was the sort of simple meal she most enjoyed and involved little effort or washing-up. She finished with ground coffee and a couple of the handmade chocolates Barry had given her. Having guessed what was in the inexpertly wrapped box, she had already opened it. The rest of her presents she saved until after lunch.

From her mother was a beautiful tan shawl threaded with gold, and the usual cheque from her father who was never sure what, to buy his adult daughter. Her parents had always sent separate gifts.

'I don't believe it.' Rose shook her head. Laura had given her earrings almost identical to the ones she had bought for Laura; made of silver filigree with an amber stone, they were the work of a local craftsman. Still, their tastes had always been similar.

With one of her new novels and the last glass of

champagne, Rose settled down on the settee. There had been no hardship in spending the day alone. In fact, she had thoroughly enjoyed it.

Maddy Duke spent Boxing Day morning in the few feet which served as her kitchen. She gave a brief thought to the police who would be working over the holidays and realised how other people's tragedies took second place at such times of the year. With her preparations well advanced and the afternoon to look forward to, it was as if Jenny Manders had never been.

When everything was ready she put on the green velvet dress she had found in a charity shop. It had a lace collar like a child's party frock but it suited her. She untied her hair and brushed it until it crackled with static then stepped into her lace-up ankle boots and waited nervously for her guests to arrive.

They all seemed to come at the same time but it pleased her to see them mingling and chatting amicably, all suspicions temporarily put on hold.

'I'm glad you could make it,' Maddy said to Rose, kissing her cheek. Her eyes glowed with gratitude. Rose Trevelyan had enabled her to express all that she had bottled up for so long. 'This is Peter Dawson,' she added with a touch of pride.

'I admire your work,' Rose said, which was true, although she preferred representational art over abstract.

'Thank you. From what I hear you're no slouch yourself.' Rose had not known what to expect, but certainly not this sophisticated, urbane man in his mid to late fifties. 'I have to admit I don't know your work,' he added.

You will, Rose thought, but did not say, hoping that Maddy's interest in Peter would divert her away from Nick who, she suspected, was not the stable person Maddy required.

'Jenny loved parties,' Maddy said, blushing because she wished she hadn't. Now was not the time to bring up her name.

Rose looked up and happened to see Nick across the room engaged in conversation with Stella. He nodded in her direction, his face grim, then, making one last comment, left Stella and approached her. 'Are you feeling better?'

'Yes, thanks. It was one of those twenty-four hour things.'

'I didn't see you there, Rose. You look lovely.' Stella had joined them.

'Thank you.' She had hoped she would not be over-dressed in a velvet skirt and a slinky blouse. Next to Stella, of course, no one would appear to be so. Today the ensemble was a black satin trouser suit enlivened by a chain belt which dipped over her narrow hips and lots of chunky costume jewellery.

'No wonder you got ill, with all that's been going on. You were probably run down. And the police. Are they leaving you alone now?'

'Yes. Why should they be doing otherwise?'

'Honestly, Rose, it stands to reason. You were the one who led them to that unfortunate girl. Ah, excuse me, I must have a word with someone.'

Rose watched her walk across the room to a couple she did not know. Too late Stella had seen her mistake and knew that Rose had seen it too. 'Nick, was it you who mentioned my idiotic panicking at the mine to Stella?' Rose had not doubted that everyone would know eventually but a thought had crossed her mind and she was interested to know exactly when Stella had heard.

'No. There was no reason to. Why?'

'I just wondered.'

Maddy had been watching this interaction with interest. Unable to paint herself, she still had a genuine interest in art and all its forms. And since that embarrassing encounter with Nick and what had followed with Rose, she had begun to see the man she thought she had been in love with in a different light. 'I hear you've finished the engine house. I'd love to see it.'

'Then you must come over one day.'

'Really? Thanks.'

Peter Dawson had not moved away. He was fascinated by the two women, who seemed to share some secret understanding.

'I wonder what it'd look like if you painted it again?' Maddy continued.

Rose frowned her lack of comprehension.

'I mean now. After what's happened. Would it affect your view of the place? I suppose what I'm trying to say is how much of what an artist sees is what's really there and how much depends on other stimuli?'

It was an interesting point. 'I think moods can

affect the way you work. A scene might well come out differently if you painted it twice; once in a happy frame of mind and again when depressed. It would reflect more in the colours than anything else, I think.' How would that landscape look, Rose wondered, knowing what I know now? 'It's a good idea, Maddy. I just might try it again, although obviously from a different perspective. Perhaps even tomorrow.' Fully aware of the people who were listening and those who were not, she thought this might be one way to find out what was going on. But it was a good idea. Painted from the opposite side and with the hills in the background instead of the engine house outlined against the sky, it would be completely different. Jack's words unheeded, Rose did not stop to think that she might be putting herself in danger, that if someone who thought she knew too much was in the room then she would have given them the perfect opportunity to remove her from the scene.

The party was beginning to break up when Rose's taxi arrived at five. The food had been eaten and enough drink consumed and conversations were beginning to flag. Only the few, like Rose, who had spent a quiet Christmas Day had the stamina to continue. But Rose had had enough socialising and was ready to leave. She thanked Maddy and said her goodbyes.

Climbing into the front seat of the taxi, the better to gossip with the driver, she realised she had been a coward. She had intended to treat Nick normally but all she had done was to avoid him.

Having met the famous, or possibly infamous, Peter

Dawson, Rose mentioned this to the driver, who was impressed. 'I thought he was virtually a hermit,' he commented.

'Reclusive, certainly, but he does come out and show his face now and again. In fact, he's coming to my New Year's Eve party.'

'We are moving up in the world. I take it you're going straight home?'

'Yes. Didn't I say?'

'No. And I'm not a mind reader. Here, did you know the girl who was killed?'

'Yes.'

'Ah. I'm sorry, Rose.'

After that there was no more conversation until they reached the bottom of her drive. Rose wished he hadn't mentioned Jenny.

The house was warm and welcoming and pleasantly quiet after the noise of the party. The light on the answering machine glowed steadily. There were no messages.

Rose kicked off her high-heeled shoes and switched on the television. An hour of viewing which required no thought would be welcome. She sat, her legs tucked beneath her, in the corner of the settee, her eyes on the screen. Later, she was unable to recall the programme that was on. All she could think about was Jenny and her friends.

Aware that Stella and Daniel, Nick, Maddy and Peter Dawson had all heard her say she intended going out to the mine again, she was not sure if she actually had the nerve to do so. And, more to the point, did she have the nerve to go back to St Ives and ask the questions that were worrying away at the back of her mind?

But where to start? She did not have a counterpart to Doreen Clarke there who knew everyone and all their business. Unless, she thought, she could rely on Maddy who saw all and said little.

# CHAPTER NINE

There had been a meeting between Jack Pearce, his chief inspector and the superintendent and the conclusion drawn from it was that Jack's theory was more than worth a try. The forensic tests were still under way and the results not expected for several days. And now the Met was involved. Elimination, they said, was often as vital as hard evidence, and that was where the London lot could help them.

Over the holiday period only a skeleton forensic team were on duty in the lab they used. This would slow things down further but the results were useless unless they were accurate.

27th December. There were four days until Rose's party. Jack had optimistically told himself that at least one of the cases might be solved by then and he would be free to attend.

All Jack's hopes were now pinned on forensic evidence, but he knew how long he'd have to wait for it.

Several divisions had already come back with negative

faxes regarding the identity of the first victim but there were still many to go. The reinterviewing of the suspects had provided little that was new except that it was now certain that Daniel Wright had had an affair with Jenny and his wife had known about it. Questioned individually, each had admitted it. The affair had been over for some time and although it gave them each a motive Jack thought it more likely that if Stella had been insanely jealous she would have acted immediately and if Daniel had been afraid of being found out he would not have confessed voluntarily. Still, sometimes emotions could simmer beneath the surface before they finally erupted.

Rose had been wrong, it seemed. Stella and Daniel swore they had been together after the preview. He did not want them to be guilty; he wanted Nick Pascoe to be the culprit because he was the most likely candidate and for a reason to which he did not care to admit. But that still leaves the problem of the first woman, he realised, then cursed for the lack of available evidence.

'I'll do it.' Rose stood in her sitting room window, much as she did every morning of her life. Having decided to let the weather dictate her movements she had no option but to go ahead. But this time I'll be prepared, she told herself. She was almost certain she knew who was trying to frighten her and, if this assumption was correct, then it was not the same person who had killed Jennifer Manders, in which case she would not be in any real danger.

A flawless blue sky stretched into the distance and the water in the bay sparkled beneath it. Many fishermen were heading out to sea. Having landed just before Christmas they could not afford to waste good weather now.

Her resolve unwavering, Rose set off with her painting equipment.

In jeans, sweatshirt and a body warmer the chill in the air ought not to penetrate. And there was always her waxed jacket which lived on the back seat of the car. Her hair was tied back firmly to prevent it blowing forward on to her palette which she tended to hold high up and close to her body. As she drove she wondered if someone would be there ahead of her.

She parked and got out of the car. There was no one in sight and nothing different about the place yet Rose felt uneasy. She walked around the engine house, her hand shielding her eyes from the low winter sun as she planned from which angle to paint it. Glancing back, she checked how far away the car was if she needed to get to it in a hurry. It was unlocked. There would be no fumbling with the key.

The rocks cast strange shadows, but Rose was not afraid of shadows. She took out a sketchpad and soft pencil and drew a few lines. After forty minutes nothing had happened and only once had she been disturbed by a rustling in the undergrowth, which was too low to contain anything other than wildlife. Why then was she suddenly afraid? The hairs on the nape of her neck prickled. She turned her head slowly. There was nothing to see her but the rolling countryside, the boulders and the bracken and a crow wheeling in the sky. Had she heard someone approaching? People knew where she was, would know where to look if anything happened to her, but they were the wrong people and by that time it would be too late. How stupid she was to have come. Breathing deeply, she steadied herself. If she was in danger it was no good falling apart, she must be prepared. The winter sun was now lower still and made her squint. It was time to go home. She stood and stretched. More time had passed than she realised. Nothing was going to happen now.

'Rose?' The voice reverberated in the thin air.

'Jesus!' Instantly she froze. Her body was rigid, every muscle tense. Unable to move, she was close to hysteria. Then, just as quickly, her limbs took on a strange quality of fluidity as if they had turned from steel to blancmange. Adrenalin pumped through her veins and dictated movement. With a dry mouth and thudding heart she grabbed her belongings and ran towards the car, flinging everything in ahead of her haphazardly.

There was a rustling and someone grabbed her arm. She screamed. This time it was her own voice which echoed in the still air.

'My God, woman! I'm not that bad.'

It was seconds before she realised that Peter Dawson, who had jumped back in alarm, was standing a yard or so away, staring at her as if she was mad – which, indeed, she felt she was at that moment. What was he doing there? But he couldn't have been the one to frighten her previously because they had not met until Maddy's get-together. Until that day he had probably never heard of her. Rose saw the utter stupidity in having gone there alone. She took a deep breath. Her heart was pounding so loudly that she thought Peter must hear it too.

'Okay, so why so terrified?' He stood with his arms folded revealing the threadbare elbows of his mustard-coloured needle-cord jacket.

Rose shook her head. Fright had rendered her speechless.

'Do you want to walk for a minute to steady your nerves, or would you rather sit down?'

'Sit,' Rose managed to say.

'Let me take your arm.' This time he gave her warning. His touch was gentle as he led her to an outcrop of rock, smooth enough upon which to sit. 'What happened? The minute I called your name you took off as if the devil himself was after you.'

'It was your fault. I didn't see you. You scared the living daylights out of me.' She was trembling from head to foot.

'Look, I don't think you're up to talking yet. Why don't we find a pub and I'll buy you a drink, or coffee, or whatever you want.'

'Thank you.' It sounded like a good idea. And at least there would be other people around. Then it struck her. 'How did you get here? Where did you come from?'

'I drove, of course. How else? And there's another way in over there.' Peter pointed. Rose, peering into the distance, saw only deep shadows and realised why she had not seen him. 'I called at your place first hoping to change your mind about coming out here. I may not intermingle much but I still hear what goes on. It was a stupid risk to take. I wanted to dissuade you.'

Rose looked around and Peter interpreted her bewilderment. 'I'm parked out on the verge. I know you can see the engine house from the road but I had no idea there was access to it by car. I imagined it would've been fenced off for safety reasons. Anyway, you follow me. I'll go slowly. Okay?'

He escorted her back to the car and walked on ahead to his own, which was some way away – this explained why Rose had not been disturbed by the sound of its engine, But her instincts had been working overtime. She *had* known there was someone there. She drove automatically, letting Peter set the pace.

They came to the St Ives junction where Rose assumed Peter would indicate to turn off but he continued on past it. Who cares? She thought, the nearer home for me the better. The roads were quiet in that no man's land of post-Christmas and pre-New Year. A cattle truck lumbered towards them, the driver's visor down against the increasingly lowering sun. In the distance the purple clouds of evening were already building up. On they went, Rose keeping a respectable distance behind Peter although she could have driven faster now. They were in Penzance before he stopped, parking on the sea front where couples and family groups strolled and children rode their new bikes or sailed past on rollerblades. The tide was in and was slapping against the sea wall with a gentle suction. Droplets of spray flew over the railings. Rose locked the car and inhaled deeply, breathing away the last of her fear, calm enough now to appreciate the sharp, clean air in her lungs.

'The Navy's open,' Peter said, looking both ways for traffic before taking Rose's arm and guiding her across the road. 'I shall make do with a soft drink but you need something stronger. You can always leave your car where it is.'

The wind was stiffening. Rose shivered and wondered whether she was about to cry. Kindness sometimes did that to her. Turning the corner she saw the boards advertising all-day opening and bar food. She had eaten there with Jack; the portions were very generous.

They sat in a corner away from the bar because there were customers whom Rose knew and she was not up to making small talk. A tape was playing which meant their conversation could not be overheard. She accepted gratefully the rather large brandy Peter had ordered for her without consultation.

'Right. What was that all about back there?'

Rose told him, her embarrassment no less acute for having repeated the story several times before.

Peter stroked his chin thoughtfully. 'Mm. I had heard much the same thing, although not quite as concise an account of it. It puzzled me that you'd want to go back there after what they found. Good heavens, Rose, it couldn't have been whoever killed that unknown victim, could it? Maybe they didn't want anyone snooping around the area.'

'I was hardly snooping.'

'No. And it was a stupid idea. The last thing they'd do

is to draw attention to it. Forget I said it. No one knew she was down there, you couldn't have done any harm just painting.' He rubbed his chin thoughtfully. 'Then that means there has to be another reason.'

'That's not what the police think.'

'They're not infallible, Rose. Tell me, what do you think?'

'I agree with you. Peter, tell me honestly, why were you there?'

'I have been honest. I heard what you said yesterday at Maddy's and the way you made a point of letting everyone know where you'd be. After you left I heard a lot more. Two unexplained murders and a middle-aged lady – who, if you don't mind me saying, looks nowhere near her age – hearing voices and intending to return to a place where she is likely to be in danger. Apart from that, an instinct told me this same lady and Maddy Duke are keeping some great secret. I was concerned for your safety, no more than that. And as far as I know there seems to be no one else to look out for you. I've also been informed that you have a knack of landing yourself in trouble. Does that explanation satisfy you?'

'It'll have to, but I didn't know you cared.' Rose bit her lip. 'I'm sorry. Forgive me, that was extremely rude.'

'It's shock. I wouldn't have put you down as rude. Outspoken, certainly, and with a excess of curiosity, but not rude.' He sipped his grapefruit juice and pulled a face. Sitting with one elbow on the table, his chin in his hand, he studied Rose's profile.

She was aware of his scrutiny and felt like a girl on

her first date. 'Let me buy you another drink,' she said decisively, anxious to escape his gaze and what it was doing to her.

'No. Really. You have one if you like. I'll wait until I'm home and can have a taste of the real thing.'

'I'll leave it in that case. I'm already feeling a bit light-headed.'

'If you're not up to walking, I can give you a lift.'

'Thank you. I'd be very grateful.' Peter was the right age to have been involved with the girl down the mine and it wouldn't surprise her if he had known Jenny as more than a friend. It was only an impression, but Rose guessed that Peter Dawson was something of what her father would describe as a 'ladies' man'. He certainly had charisma and charm. He might not mix much but she sensed a warm personality behind the outward persona, and she found she was interested in what he had to say.

'Is it serious between you and Nick?' he asked as they made their way back to his car.

'A relationship that doesn't exist can hardly be described as serious,' she told him solemnly.

'Ah.'

'Ah, what?'

'Just interested. Rose, please don't think I'm an interfering old fool, but be careful of Nick.'

'In what way?'

'It's hard to say. I've known him a good many years now. He's talented, extremely so, but he has a touch of the artistic temperament.'

'People use that as an excuse for bad behaviour.' They

stood at the kerb. A line of cars approached from both directions.

'Do they? It hadn't occurred to me. Perhaps I had better look to some of my own bad habits. I don't mean he's a threat to you, it's just that he's never settled down. I think Jenny was the longest relationship he's ever had.'

'You're not married or living with anyone.'

'No. But I'm different.' He laughed when he saw Rose's cynical grimace. 'Of course, we all like to think that. But I know I have no staying power. The women I meet, and please don't take offence, bore me within a very short time. It's a lack in me, not them, you understand. I enjoy being solitary, I love not having to worry about anything other than my work. I walk or paint or read or eat Or drink whenever the mood takes me. It would take a very unusual woman to put up with my selfishness. Yes,' he said, as if it had only just occurred to him, 'that's what it is. I won't allow myself to be changed or to fit in with anyone else's plans.'

There was a gap in the traffic and they were able to cross the road. Rose guessed he was saying it for her benefit, that he had known his faults for many years.

'I'm a little like that myself these days.'

'It must've been hard, losing your husband.'

'There are no words to describe what I felt. You see, we were lucky, our marriage worked. We sort of, I don't know, fitted each other.'

'Children?'

'None, but it didn't seem to matter. Anyway, since then I've pleased myself too.' She smiled and was rewarded with a conspiratorial grin. 'I have to admit I have the same problem with men. Not that there've been many, but the few I've met have tried to pin me down. They're possessive. David wasn't like that, we each had our own lives as well as each other.'

'Then I doubt you'll find a replacement.'

'I don't intend to.'

Peter bent to unlock the car and they got in. 'Nick isn't possessive, not in the usual way,' he continued. 'He'd allow you freedom, but he'd want to know how you used it. Does that make sense?'

'Peter?' Rose looked at him steadily. 'Could he have killed Jenny?'

'That idea has crossed my mind. However, the police haven't arrested him.'

'They suspect me, too.'

'So I had heard.'

'Do you think it's true?'

'My judgement is not always infallible, Rose, but if you killed Jenny Manders then I'm the Queen Mother.'

'Thank you,' she said with such warmth that she felt tears of relief behind her eyelids.

'Now we'd better make tracks. Do up your seat belt.'

'What do you mean about Nick? Apart from his being a little possessive?'

'He can be moody. He likes his own way. God, we're a selfish lot when you think about it. He doesn't believe women are equal and, apart from Jenny who was far stronger than most people gave her credit for, he'll bleed you dry emotionally if you let him.'

'Do you believe women are equal?' Rose was fascinated to learn that she was more interested in Peter Dawson's personality at that moment than Nick's.

'There's nothing to believe. All men are equal, and I use that term figuratively. It's not something I've come to a decision about, I've always known it. You only have to look around you. In some situations it's the female who keeps things going and in others the male. My own parents were a perfect example of the former.'

Rose would have liked to ask in what way but they had reached Newlyn and Peter was taking the sharp bend on the bridge and she did not wish to distract him. He dropped her at the bottom of her drive and made no attempt to get her to invite him in.

'Take care, Rose,' he said through the open window of the car.

'I will.'

I need something to eat, she decided, and began to arrange the ingredients for something quick and easy. Pasta with a bacon, tomato and garlic sauce. The onions were sweating and their mouthwatering smell made Rose aware just how hungry she was. As she slid them around the pan she thought of Nick. His moodiness had not gone unobserved. How much more pronounced would it have become if she had got to know him better? He had a temper, too, although he kept it hidden.

Lying in bed she listened to the wind and the familiar sounds of the house settling down: the creak of a stair, the ticking of the heating system as it cooled and the hum of the washing machine as it reached the end of its cycle.

She had spoken to Maddy, who had been able to provide some of the information Rose wanted. It was certainly food for thought. But for now there was the party to think of and the less metaphorical sort of food to consider.

# CHAPTER TEN

'Oh, to hell with it.' Inspector Jack Pearce scowled at the wall. Missing Rose was one thing, his personal decision not to contact her was another. There was nothing in the rule book to prevent him speaking to her, only his own sense of what was right. What he wanted, what he had hoped for was that Rose, in her distress, would contact him, use his shoulder to lean on. He had forgotten how perversely stubborn she could be.

Each of Jenny's friends had had the opportunity and possibly the motive to kill her but, as motives went, they were not strong. He was ashamed to admit that if Rose were not involved he would have taken it in his stride. It was, after all, what he was trained to do. If only there were some easy solution. Mostly there was, he thought, it was knowing where to look for it which was the hard part.

The forensic team was continuing its assiduous work and would not be hurried. Jack knew better than to pester them, it often provoked a slower response.

Against his better judgement he decided he would speak

to Rose after all. Apart from an edge to the wind, it was a lovely day. He telephoned first because Rose might be taking advantage of it. He wanted to hear her theory – that she would have one he was in no doubt – but he had to be content to leave a message on her answering machine.

Towards the end of the day another piece of evidence was to hand. The Met had confirmed that the woman they had been asked to interview had not been seen for several days but they were continuing in their efforts to find her. Rather than disappointment, Jack felt only relief. This proved that he was on the right lines.

Feeling the need for a quiet evening in, Jack was about to leave for home when Rose returned his call. His spirits lifted until she spoke.

'I got your message. Is this business or pleasure?'

'A bit of both. Are you doing anything this evening?'

'Yes. Laura's coming over to help with the food.'

'The food? Oh, your party. Never mind, it wasn't important.'

'Will you be coming, Jack?'

'Is that a devious way of asking if an arrest is imminent?' Her light laugh cheered him; her initial words had sounded hostile.

'Well, is it?'

'No. But hopefully it won't be long.' Jack could almost feel her curiosity oozing down the line and pictured the furrow which dissected her forehead when she frowned with frustration.

'I wonder if you're thinking along the same lines as me?'

'Rose . . . ?'

'Sorry, Jack. Must go. Laura's here.' Only when she put down the phone did she remember the book Nick had so recently given to Jennifer Manders. Did Jack know that the relationship had continued long after everyone thought it was over? If she told him, Nick would think that she had been acting like a woman scorned because she had been jealous. She decided to think about it. Nick may have volunteered the information already and Jack would start doubting her loyalty to her friends. Rose wondered why that should matter any more.

'Damn the woman.' Jack was listening to the dialling tone. He slammed down the phone with a further curse, wondering what Rose was up to.


Peter Dawson was sprawled on his sofa quite unconcerned that two men were searching his cottage and packing a few of his clothes into plastic bags. He reached out and poured himself a malt whisky although it was only ten-thirty in the morning. He was quite unconcerned about that too.

'Do you always drink so early?' one of the men asked.

'If I choose to.' He smiled with a lift of an eyebrow as he read their minds.

Had Rose reported his having been at the mine or had they learnt of Jenny's visits? It did not take long to establish it was the latter.

'Why didn't you come forward at the beginning?' one of the men asked. 'We know Miss Manders used to come here.'

'Your request was for information concerning her whereabouts from after the time she left Stella Jackson's gallery. I hadn't seen her for several weeks therefore I'd have been wasting your time.' He had no objection to them poking around, there was nothing for them to find, but he was fed up with their company and he needed a chance to think. It would have been nice to stride out across the cliffs and gaze at the sea, to smell the salt and the heady scent of grass as he crushed it beneath his feet. Instead he had to go to Camborne to make a statement. Peter couldn't understand why, with two of them present, he was unable to do so in the comfort of his own home.

One of the men stared suspiciously at Peter's cassette player.

'You won't find any traces of soil or anything. I wiped it clean when I got back from the mine.'

'What?' Both men spoke in unison.

Peter laughed mirthlessly. 'Just my little attempt at humour. Please, carry on.' He waved his hand to indicate the entire contents of the room. 'I'd be grateful if you'd leave the settee.'

He felt quite tired once they had left. Fingerprints had been taken, which he had explained was also a waste of time. They had come out with their trite phrase of 'for the purposes of elimination' but all the same he knew that there would probably be some of Jenny's around the place. He looked after himself and kept the cottage clean but not to such an extent that he went around wiping paintwork. He had already admitted that Jenny had been an occasional visitor but they had gone ahead with their dust anyway. He threw the receipt for the belongings they had taken on to the table.

Later that day, having abstained from drinking more whisky and substituted it with black coffee, he drove over to Camborne, arriving punctually for his appointment. The interview seemed interminably long. First there was the rigmarole of ensuring he understood what was going on then the tediousness of the questions themselves.

'How well do you know Mrs Trevelyan?' he was asked, towards the end.

Because he realised that Rose was likely to be questioned he saw no reason not to tell them that he had encountered her at the mine. Peter said he had only followed her because he was worried about her safety. Two pairs of eyebrows were raised sceptically.

'In what way were you worried, Mr Dawson? You've just said you hardly know her.'

'I don't know,' he replied truthfully. 'I just had a feeling that she oughtn't to be out there on her own.'

'An odd thing to think without a reason?'

'I didn't think, I said it was just a feeling.'

'Are you having a relationship with Mrs Trevelyan?'

'Good heavens, no.' The question shook him. It was an honest answer but they seemed not to believe him.

'But Nicholas Pascoe is.' This came out as a statement.

'No, I don't think so. As far as I'm aware they're friends, no more than that. I think you should ask the lady herself if you really need to know.'

'Are you seeing anyone at the moment?'

'Seeing anyone?' His tone was mocking.

'A girlfriend? Mistress, whatever?'

'No. Not at the moment.'

'Not since Jennifer Manders.'

Peter's jaw tightened imperceptibly. 'She was not a girlfriend. It was a very casual thing.'

'Casual?'

'Look, I told you earlier, she came to the house on a few occasions. We enjoyed each other sexually, if that's what you're after, but it was no more than that. We had nothing else in common other than a desire for sex without emotional ties.'

'That may have been your wish, Mr Dawson, but most women think differently.'

'Do they? Perhaps in your experience, not in mine. I'm sure you'll find I was not alone in having a quick tumble with her.'

'Meaning what?'

'I suggest you ask around. My word is only hearsay and that, I believe, is not permissible evidence. Now, your men have ransacked my home, taken away certain of my possessions, and I've spent enough of the afternoon here. I would like to leave now.'

'You are perfectly free to do so, sir. Just one more question? If you're so keen to be emotionally free of women, maybe Miss Manders became more demanding than you cared for. Did you kill her?'

Peter sighed. 'No. I did not kill Jennifer Manders.'

'Thank you. Someone'll show you out.'

When he left he felt restless. A walk on the cliffs was out of the question now. It would be dark before he reached home and, as there was no moon, it would be foolhardy to risk the narrow path so close to the edge. Perhaps he would get blind drunk and wash the awfulness of the day from his system. On the other hand he could ring Rose Trevelyan to compare notes. This he did from a public telephone box before deciding whether it was worth going home. She answered on the second ring as if she had been waiting for a call. But not from him.

'Peter? Where are you?' Rose could hear background noises which she guessed were traffic.

'In a call box. I need some TLC. I have been grilled by the police. They tied me to a chair and shone a bright light in my eyes and whipped me with wet towels until I begged for mercy and confessed.' He was gratified to hear her laughing. 'So is there any chance of us meeting for a drink or dinner?' He was surprised to find himself holding his breath while she made up her mind.

'Not tonight, I'm getting ready for the 31st.' She hesitated briefly then added, 'But I'm free tomorrow.'

'Fine. What time shall I pick you up?'

'Oh, seven-thirty?'

Turning the car around he realised how much he was looking forward to it. There was nothing run-of-the-mill about Mrs Trevelyan, he thought as he headed for home.

Rose's head was spinning. Another man wants to take me out? she thought, returning to the kitchen. Laura's suggestive smirk didn't help. 'You've got flour in your hair,' Rose told her acidly.

'Perhaps you'd better take a look in the mirror yourself, girl.'

They had been enjoying themselves, wrist deep in pastry

dough as they prepared the cases for flans. Wine glasses stood near to hand, their bases dusted with flour, their stems smeared with greasy fingerprints. At least with Laura Rose could avoid the topic of Jenny Manders.

'For a woman who, not many days since, was crying into her beer over the inadequacies of men and who vowed to have nothing more to do with them, you're doing a fine impression of exactly the opposite. You're on the phone to Jack when I get here and less than an hour later someone called Peter rings up. That's two, without Nick.'

'Oh, honestly, Laura!' Rose made as if to slap her arm and knocked over the bag of flour. A small cloud of it settled on them both and they collapsed laughing.

'Rose?' Laura, who was facing the window, frowned over her shoulder.

Rose turned around. 'What is it?'

'God, I'm getting as bad as you. For a second I thought I saw someone out there. It was probably my own reflection.'

Rose went to the door and opened it. The sloping garden and drive were deserted. There was nothing but the bone-like rattle of the leafless trees as the wind lifted the boughs. Out in the bay the lights of three trawlers winked as they followed each other in procession. The chug, chug of their engines carried clearly across the expanse of water. 'There's no one there,' Rose said, closing the door again. She made them both supper while they waited for the flan bases to bake.

Spearing omelette on to her fork, Laura watched Rose surreptitiously. 'Okay, out with it, what's bothering you? Did you really think there was someone out there?'

'I don't know. I went over to St Ives today. They all seem to have hang-ups of some description.'

'By that you mean your arty friends?'

'Yes. But I can't believe one of them's a murderer.'

'Can't, or won't?'

'You're right. I won't. But I have been thinking about it and they all seem to have had something to gain by killing Jenny, even if it doesn't amount to much. But for the life of me I can't understand why there's so much mystery attached to the other body. I mean, surely someone knows who it is? I was convinced it was Renata Manders but it seems I was wrong.'

'It could be absolutely anyone. Not everyone's lucky enough to have people who'll miss them.'

'I know.'

'Rose, at the risk of sounding like Barry Rowe, leave it to Jack. I know there's something going through your pretty little head. If there is, tell him. Oh, God.' Laura jumped up, suddenly remembering the pastry which they could now smell.

Her hands encased in oven gloves, Rose lifted several fluted-sided dishes from the oven. She had borrowed some from Laura. 'Thank goodness you remembered. That was just in time.'

'On the other hand,' Laura continued, ignoring the results of their work, 'if you think you know something you really ought to tell Jack.'

'I know.' But Rose suspected Jack was ahead of her and that all he wanted was some conclusive evidence.

'But you want to solve it all yourself. I can tell by that

grin that you're dying to show him what a clever girl you are.'

'Yes. Now are you going to help with the fillings or are you rushing off home now that I've fed and watered you?'

'That depends.'

'On what?' Rose followed the direction of Laura's gaze. 'I never was lucky in my choice of friends,' she said, reaching for the corkscrew.

After Laura had left Rose cleared up the kitchen and surveyed the food laid out on the worktops to cool. There was probably too much of it but some could be left in the freezer until the last minute.

Physically tired from her achievements in the kitchen but still on a high mentally from an idea that had crept into her mind, she was not quite ready for bed. She poured the last glass of wine, went through to the sitting room and settled into the chair which faced the one where David had always sat and where she often pictured him.

Over the telephone she had asked Maddy if she knew of any of Renata's friends. Maddy had not been in the area very long but she seemed to soak up information like a sponge. And she had been close to Jenny who talked a lot.

'Jenny told me the name of one. She had a vague memory of her from when she was little but mainly because she was forbidden to go near her by her father. Alec said she was a bad influence on Renata. Anyway, Jenny always thought there had been something going on between her father and this woman.'

'What's her name?' Rose had asked impatiently.

'Josie Deveraux. At least, it was, she might have married.'

Rose had written it down, disappointed when Maddy went on to say, 'She moved away ages ago.'

Sitting quietly at the end of a long day Rose felt extremely sorry for Renata Manders. Her domineering mother-in-law had alienated her from her family and she had been more or less forbidden to see what may have been her only friend.

When Rose had gone to St Ives that morning she found the house where Josie Deveraux used to live was now inhabited by an elderly couple who had never heard of her. She realised now that even if they had done so they were hardly likely to have answered the questions of a complete stranger.

Why she wanted to know about the Deveraux woman, Rose wasn't sure, except it stemmed from her innate curiosity which would not be satisfied until she knew the whole story.

She had hoped the two women had kept in touch. Deep down she wanted to hear that, if it wasn't Renata they had found, things had worked out for her, that she was now happy.

Rose's head ached. A dull thudding behind her temples made her nauseous. It was time for bed.

By morning her headache was worse. Rose regretted acceding to Laura's wishes by opening the second bottle of wine. There was a heavy stillness in the air which did not help. As she watched, the grey canopy of the sky became sulphurous and then darkened. She realised that it was the weather rather than the wine which was responsible for how she felt. The bitter scent of the narcissi filled the room just as the first flash of lightning crackled over the bay. Seconds later thunder crashed and seemed to shake the house. The rain came suddenly, hammering down. Storms such as this had been known to roll around the bay for hours on end. Rose had intended going to Penzance to try to find something to wear for her party but for the moment it was impossible to go out.

The storm died down around eleven and the rain eased a little. She gave it half an hour then picked up her car keys and left the house.

The traffic was heavy and she joined the slow crawl up through Market Jew Street where buses were at the stops on both sides of the road causing further delays.

Her expedition was unsuccessful. Being a size eight and only five feet two inches tall, Rose was swamped by most modern fashions. She put it down to the after-effects of the headache which made her feel uneasy, but she had the impression that something was wrong.

As she turned into her drive she noticed a van parked across the road. The driver's face was turned away but she still recognised him. She quickly locked the car and went into the house, also locking the kitchen door, something she rarely did unless she was going out. Her heart was racing. Had she been right all along? She rang Jack immediately. Aware that she was gabbling she wondered if Jack had any idea what she was talking about.

'Stay there. Don't move,' he told her. 'I'm on my way.'

Minutes later there was a knock on the kitchen door. For a second Rose was filled with relief. It was too soon for Jack to have arrived but Laura had said she might call in with some paper plates and serviettes she had left over from her own Christmas preparations.

But on the other side of the glass stood Alec Manders, rain running down his face. 'Let me in,' he mouthed.

Rose froze, mentally urging Jack to drive faster. She backed out into the hall, terrified by the anger in the man's face. If she got to the front door she could reach the side of the house unseen and come out further down the drive below him. Then she would have a chance of making it to the road before he realised what was happening.

'Oh, God.' Her voice was hoarse. She had heard glass breaking. The key was on the inside of the kitchen door. If she had had the sense to remove it Alec Manders would have had to smash the wood which supported the four panes and she would have had more time.

In one movement she reached the front door and unlocked it. Grabbing the round, brass handle and the flat metal plate of the Yale, she heaved. The door didn't budge. So recently she had broken a nail doing this and promised to do something about it. More rain had swollen the wood further. It was too late now.

'Mrs Trevelyan.' His voice was low and controlled and therefore all the more terrifying. 'Why are you asking questions about me?'

He wanted to talk. Maybe that was all he wanted. 'I'm not.'

'You've been speaking to people in St Ives. You bothered an old couple who live near me. And you came to my house to offer your condolences which was just an excuse to poke your nose into my business. I know what you're thinking and it isn't true. And you're not the only one. I didn't kill my wife. She left me, you stupid bitch.'

Something about his words struck a chord. He had not denied killing Jenny. 'Why did you break in?' Rose knew she must keep him talking.

'So *you'd* know what it feels like to have your privacy invaded. You're in the phone book, it wasn't hard to find you. What were you doing out at the mine?'

She knew then that she was right. Alec Manders, most probably through Jenny, had learnt that she was working there. 'Painting.'

'Painting.' His voice was scornful as he took a step nearer.

She had her back to the door. To her left was a small table which held a plant pot. Beside it was an old walking-stick stand. All it contained was an umbrella. Rose reached for it as Alec simultaneously reached for her. She felt the heat of his breath on her face and, as she tried to swing away and he grabbed at her hair, she thought how clean he smelt.

There was a jolt of pain in her back. Opening her eyes Rose realised that she was on the floor, that what she had felt was herself falling. Alec was on top of her, one knee pressed into her stomach, pinning her down. The pain made her want to vomit. 'I didn't want to have to do this,' she heard him say from a distance. 'But I didn't kill Renata.'

Weakly she raised her hand and brought the umbrella down on his head. It was the most ineffectual thing she had done in her life. It bounced off his thick hair causing him to jeer. 'I don't think so, Mrs Trevelyan.' He wrenched it from her and threw it down the hall, his knee still in place. Above Rose's head the ceiling began to swim as she struggled for breath. 'You're coming with me,' he said, pulling her to her feet. Rose tried to kick out at his shins but he twisted her arm behind her. She felt it might snap. There's still a chance, she thought, he hasn't killed me yet and I don't think he'll do it here. I've got to play for time, to give Jack a chance to get here. She was convinced that her destiny also lay in that mine shaft.

There was glass all over the kitchen floor from where Alec had stuck his elbow through the pane. It scrunched beneath the soles of Rose's boots. They had almost reached the door but Alec pushed her sharply against the edge of the sink, her arm still bent behind her. With his spare hand he rummaged in drawers, cursing when he couldn't find what he was looking for.

He has to tie me up, Rose realised. He has to do that before he can go and fetch the van. There was string upstairs, and whole rolls of strong cord with which she hung her pictures. Would he think of that? It would use up more time, he would have to take her up there with him, time in which Jack might arrive. Part of her mind was listening for cars but none had slowed. She sensed Alec was losing control of his temper. He yanked harder at her arm and she screamed in agony. 'There's string upstairs,' she told him, unable to help herself. She would do anything to make the pain stop.

Halfway up the stairs she stumbled. What if Jack wasn't coming? What if he was so fed up with her he couldn't be bothered or he had decided she was making a fuss about nothing again? Tears were rolling down her face and her nose began to run. If he did turn up she vowed she would never, ever be horrible to him again.

A car door slammed and was echoed by another. Downstairs there was a noise, quite a lot of noise, Rose thought.

'Let her go.' Jack took the stairs two at a time and twisted Alec around to face him. Rose fell awkwardly on the stair above but not before she had seen Jack raise his fist.

'Sir!' DS Green grabbed Alec's hands, one then the other, and encircled his wrists with the cuffs he had pulled from his pocket. He turned to Jack with a glare. 'It's just as well you didn't,' he said.

Jack nodded. He had nearly lost it there, had almost broken the rule about least possible restraint, and all because of Rose Trevelyan. 'Take him out to the car,' he said gruffly, reaching for Rose's arm.

Rose winced, staring at Jack uncomprehendingly as he got her upright with far more force than was necessary. Instead of gratitude she felt only disappointment. Hadn't she just provided the necessary evidence for them to arrest the murderer? Why did she always rub Jack up the wrong way?

There were two uniformed officers downstairs. One offered to make Rose a cup of tea. 'Thank you.' She sat at the kitchen table, trembling. Jack ignored her until the tea was in front of her. 'Tell us what happened,' he said. 'Not your assumptions or any wild guesswork, just the facts as they relate to today.'

Rose did so, wishing she had a chance to show him she had been right. It did not take long.

'Thank you. Now I suggest if Laura Penfold is busy you get your good friend Barry Rowe to come over.'

The way he spoke Barry's name made Rose cringe. Inspector Jack Pearce could be truly obnoxious when he chose. 'He'll be delighted,' she said spitefully, already having forgotten her earlier vow.

'Come on.' Jack nodded to the man who had made the tea, indicating that it was time to go. 'And ring someone to take care of this,' he added, pointing to the broken pane. 'We've got to go. Your other friend, Mr Pascoe, has just been arrested.'

'What?' She looked startled. 'You bastard,' she hissed loudly enough for Jack to hear as he walked away. As he closed the door firmly another shard of glass fell to the floor.

# CHAPTER ELEVEN

On the last morning of the year Rose began to lay out the food and drink for the party, which no longer seemed like a good idea. Since Alec Manders had broken into her house there had been no word from Jack, officers she did not know had taken her statement. Nor was there any further news of Nick.

With all that had happened she wondered how many people would turn up. Certainly not Jenny and Nick and, by his silence, not Jack either. That a man had been arrested for the murder of Jennifer Manders had been given out on the news, that his name had been withheld was irrelevant. Everybody locally knew it was Nick.

Alec's attack upon Rose convinced her that he had known of the presence of the woman in the mine shaft even if he hadn't put her there. Why else would he have been so angry and determined to stop Rose asking further questions?

I must forget it, she told herself. She had been way out in her calculations and was relieved now that she had not had a chance to mention them to Jack.

Tomorrow was the start of another year, one she would be entering with the loss of three friends. Jenny was dead, Nick in prison and Jack had finally abandoned her. The last, she thought, was no more than she deserved yet this loss hurt her most of all.

At lunch time she walked down to Newlyn to buy the olives she had forgotten. What does Peter Dawson make of me? she thought as she stopped to count the fishing-boats in the harbour.

She had cancelled their dinner date after Alec's unwelcome visit but had offered no explanation.

It was a mild day and the smell of fish hung in the air. Rose returned with the olives, reassured by the sight of her car in the drive. It had been returned as promised a week ago with the cursory comment that it would not be required again. Nick's car had not been returned as far as she was aware so she could only assume the worst: it had contained incriminating evidence and that was why he had been arrested. To someone of Rose's temperament it was extremely frustrating not to know what was going on.

At six o'clock, satisfied that everything was ready, she ran a bath and tried to relax before spending some time on her hair and make-up. There was no new dress and the wardrobe didn't hold out too much promise. In the end she chose a plain black velvet dress she had had for a number of years. Around her neck was the single strand of pearls David had bought her for no other reason, he had said, than because he loved her.

By eight-thirty everyone Rose had expected had arrived, including Doreen and Cyril Clarke. Doreen was even more matronly in a tight-fitting brocade dress. 'Leave it, do,' she said to Cyril as he fidgeted with his tie. 'I like a man to look smart,' she added. Despite her views on 'they people' Doreen made it her business to speak to everyone from St Ives. Knowing she would be grilling them about their backgrounds and who they were related to caused Rose some amusement. She would be interested in Doreen's opinion of them. That she would eventually hear it was certain.

Barry had turned up with a case of champagne which he suggested they put in the freezer half an hour before midnight as it would not all fit in the fridge. Rose was taken aback. He was thoughtful and kind but not renowned for such generous gestures. 'I thought it was time I spent something of what I earned,' he told her, kissing her cheek.

Drinks were flowing and Rose had turned up the music. When she turned around her mouth dropped open. Standing in the sitting room doorway, a drink in his hand, was Nick Pascoe.

'I can see you weren't expecting me,' he said with a smile.

He looks awful, Rose thought, as if he's already served a prison sentence. It was also the first time she'd seen him dressed so smartly. He had not made the effort for Maddy's do and Rose was unsure what to make of it. Over well-cut trousers he wore a cream silk shirt and a black velvet jacket as if by way of telepathy they'd chosen matching outfits. 'They let you go? Well, obviously they did.'

'It was a mistake. In retrospect I don't blame them, there were things I should have said from the beginning.'

'What made them think it was you?' Rose blushed. Even

at her own party, the first she had hosted for many years, she still could not help interrogating a guest.

'There was blood in my car. Jenny's blood. And to make it worse it was on the back seat. It was useless trying to explain that she'd stepped on some glass when we were out one day. She never did wear shoes if she could help it. Anyway, it was a bad cut. I put her in the back of the car and told her to keep her foot up then I drove her to Treliske hospital. It required several stitches. I'd forgotten about it until now.'

Rose realised that such an injury would have shown up during the post-mortem. However, the police would not have let Nick go for that reason alone. Rose had gone over all the possibilities then turned them on their heads. None of her friends came out well in her analysis but she still doubted their guilt. Could it be that Alec Manders, who had had no compunction about smashing his way into her house and becoming violent, had killed one or both women? But what possible reason could he have for harming his own daughter? 'Well, I'm really pleased you're here, Nick.'

'Are you, Rose?'

'Yes.' She was glad, but not in the way he might have imagined. He was extremely good-looking and quite sexy with that question still lingering in his eyes, but she saw all this objectively now. She was glad but only because she had not wanted one of her friends to be guilty and, more selfishly, she had not wanted to be wrong. 'I'd better circulate. And so had you. Just look at all the curious faces.' Rose moved away before he had a chance to say anything more.

As Rose crossed the hall on her way to the kitchen to pour more drinks she saw Stella, who was on her way up to the bathroom. Her face was flushed. Rose hoped she had not drunk too much. Several minutes later, when the food was uncovered and people had been told to help themselves, there was still no sign of Stella.

Rose went upstairs and knocked on the bathroom door. 'Stella? Are you okay?'

'Yes.'

'Open the door. Please?'

Seconds later Stella did so. 'Are you ill?' Rose was shocked at the misery in her face. It was covered in red and white blotches and there were smudges of mascara under her eyes. 'Come with me,' she said, leading her to her bedroom. 'Is it Daniel? Have you had a row?'

'No.' Stella's voice was low. She sat on the edge of the bed and laced her hands. The knuckles were white. 'I don't know what I've done.'

'What do you mean?' She sat beside her. If Stella needed to talk she would not do so with Rose looming over her judgementally.

'I can't understand what comes over me at times. Oh, Rose, why can't I be happy like you?'

Rose did not answer. There was none to give. Happy? Yes, with David she had been. Then had come the cancer which had destroyed them both in different ways. Since that time she had made the best of life and had come to accept that peace was the most that she could hope for. Happy? No. But there were still moments of pleasure and times of laughter. 'Was it you, Stella? Those screams at the mine?'

231

Stella still had not lifted her head. Now her lower lip was white as she bit it. 'I'm so sorry.'

'But why? Do you dislike me that much?'

'No. No, of course I don't. I just . . . I just couldn't bear it, watching you go through something I achieved years ago. I wanted it all back; the first hint of success, the first exhibition, the first large cheque and the knowledge that the future was ahead of me. Once you're successful you lose all that. You just end up treading water to stay where you are.'

'But that's not true, Stella, each painting is a new challenge.'

'It sounds so feeble now,' Stella continued, ignoring Rose's comment, 'but I just couldn't cope with the competition. It's hard enough with Daniel.'

'Is that how you see it?'

'He's always been more talented than me, yet he's far more relaxed about it.'

Poor Stella, Rose thought. With so many self-imposed obstacles life must be extremely difficult.

'I'm back on medication again but it doesn't seem to be working this time.'

Certain things fell into place. Stella's nervous habits and the occasional lapses where her expression was vacant and she lost concentration were not due to artistic temperament but to a genuine psychiatric disorder, the cause of her mild paranoia. 'But had I not returned to the mine, what would you have achieved? I'd have painted elsewhere, Stella, you wouldn't have stopped me—' But how far would she have taken it? Rose wondered with a shudder of fear.

'That painting was so good. I knew it immediately you showed it to me even though it wasn't finished then. I thought if I could stop you this time you might lose heart.'

She really is sick, Rose realised, and she probably ought not to be drinking on top of medication but perhaps the combination had prompted the admission. 'How did you do it?'

'I got the idea from Maddy. I knew she used tapes to practise accents. I recorded my own screams, right at the end of a blank tape, then I waited until I saw your car and set it going knowing there was at least forty minutes of silence until you heard the screams. I've lived here all my life, I knew exactly where to hide. Oh, Rose, what have I done?'

Rose handed her some tissues from the box on her dressing table.

'I had no idea you'd ring for help, really I didn't.'

'But why do it again?'

'Nick told me you'd said you'd made a fool of yourself. I was certain you wouldn't call out the emergency services a second time.'

Oh, Nick, you lied to me more than once, Rose thought. He had denied telling Stella. 'Stella, tell me, did you leave the gallery that night after the preview?' She was unbalanced enough to have done anything, including killing Jenny. Being jealous of Rose's work was one thing, but being jealous of another woman in her husband's bed was another. When Stella did not answer Rose knew it was so. They had all, in their various ways, lied. She felt sick with disgust and near to tears herself. But what did any of it matter? She had done her duty by telling Jack all she knew – or, at least, most of it – and this evening was supposed to be a celebration. For a second she wished she could simply ask all of her guests, bar Barry Rowe, to leave. In Stella's case she did not have to.

'We'll go now, Rose. I think it's for the best. Will you tell the police?'

'I don't know, Stella, I honestly don't know.' And then Rose saw that not only had Stella lied about several things but she was also about the same age as the unknown female. Perhaps the whole story of wanting to damage Rose's career was a further fabrication. Had she been too trusting? Did Stella prefer to admit to a spiteful trick rather than more serious reasons for not wanting anyone in the vicinity of the mine? Rose hated the whole business.

Somehow she got through the rest of the evening. At least her guests were enjoying themselves. Laura's son had Barbara Phillips in fits of laughter and Nick Pascoe was dancing with Doreen Clarke who held herself stiffly, keeping a good three inches between her body and Nick's. Rose was tempted to go upstairs and get a camera. Laura, Maddy and Barry were in deep conversation in a corner and Peter Dawson, chatting to Mike Phillips, surveyed the room with an amused smile and winked at Rose as she carried out some paper plates. Daniel had made excuses for their early departure. No one, looking at Stella, could have doubted she felt unwell.

At midnight Barry poured the champagne and they toasted the New Year. The party finally broke up at two.

Rose could hardly go back on her offer that those wishing to stay the night could do so.

Having settled Barbara and Mike Phillips in the spare bedroom and Peter Dawson on the settee with a sleeping bag and pillow, Rose stood in the kitchen surveying the detritus and wished Jack would get in touch soon. No one had heard what had happened to Alec Manders and there had been no further news bulletins regarding an arrest for either murder. But the more Rose thought about it the more confused she became. Nick had apparently been cleared but now Stella seemed a likely candidate. Yet deep down she had a feeling that it was Alec Manders who had put the woman down that shaft.

The first to wake, Rose recalled that she was still playing the role of hostess to three of her guests. Originally Nick had been intending to stay. Last night he been polite and friendly but had left around one. He had paid a lot of attention to Maddy but, to Rose's amazement, Maddy had treated his advances with a casual nonchalance even though she agreed to share the same taxi home. Surprisingly, considering he was supposed to be her guest, Maddy had been even more blasé about Peter Dawson staying the night.

Washing and dressing quickly to leave the bathroom free for her guests, Rose went down to make coffee and light the grill. She had never possessed a toaster. Above, floorboards creaked as someone else went to the bathroom. Ten minutes later Barbara appeared, closely followed by Mike. 'I hope you feel better than you look,' Barbara commented unkindly to her husband, holding his jaw between finger and thumb the better to scrutinise him. 'Ah, coffee. Wonderful.' They sat at the table and all three turned when Peter appeared in the doorway. He wore only his shirt and a pair of underpants. Rose felt herself blush when her eyes dropped to his long muscular legs. He seemed quite unabashed at his half-dressed state.

'I smelt the coffee,' he said, running a hand through his hair. There was reddish stubble on his chin, interspersed with silvery grey which glinted beneath the overhead light.

Rose handed them each a mug and placed the sugar bowl and milk on the table.

'Is the grill on for warmth or are we to be offered sustenance?'

Rose caught Barbara's eye. Her friend was trying not to laugh. 'Toast,' Rose snapped. 'I don't have any bacon.'

'Toast is fine.'

He had not mentioned their broken date. After the incident with Alec Manders she had only just remembered to ring him in time to prevent him setting off to meet her that evening; she had offered no excuse because she had not wished to tell a lie, but neither could she face talking about her ordeal. Barry had come over for an hour but had soon realised Rose wanted to be alone. As if the thought of him had made him materialise, he walked past the kitchen window. This time both Rose and Barbara could not suppress their grins as Barry adjusted his glasses and glared pointedly at Peter's bare legs. 'I came for the champagne glasses,' he said.

'I haven't washed them yet.'

'I'll do it.' Peter was on his feet and across the kitchen

in three strides. 'While you make some toast,' he added over his shoulder in a proprietorial tone, unaware of the impression he was making. Barry's scowl deepened.

Within fifteen minutes the glasses were in the box in which they had come from the off-licence. Barry had borrowed them free of charge on the strength of the amount of his order. The toast had been eaten and Barbara and Mike said they were leaving.

'Can I give you a lift somewhere?' Barry asked Peter rather acidly.

'No, thanks. You carry on. I'm in no hurry.'

Rose turned away, unable to face Barry because she knew what must be going through his mind.

'I'll see you soon, Rose,' he said then he, too, had gone.

'I was sorry you changed your mind about dinner,' Peter said, scooping toast crumbs towards him.

'I didn't change my mind. Unforeseen circumstances.'

He stared hard. 'Another man? Nick, maybe?'

'Another man? Yes. You could say that.' Rose sighed then sat down to give him a shortened version of that day's events.

Peter whistled through his teeth. 'I have to admit, you can't better that as a way of getting out of dinner with a man. Dare I ask if our date is still on?'

'Yes. It is.'

'Good. I'll go and make myself respectable then you can tell me when.'

What have you done now? she wondered as she wiped the work surfaces, relieving them of sticky rings of alcohol and crumbs.

'Thanks for the bed,' Peter said when he returned fully dressed. 'Here's my number. Give me a ring when you fancy going out.'

Rose nodded and took the business card he handed her then closed the door behind him, glad to be alone at last.

It was another week before Rose saw Jack. He had decided to get away, to take some leave due to him and visit his sons. The younger boy was still living with his mother in Leeds where he was, Jack had once confided in Rose, turning into a perpetual student. The older son was in Sheffield, where he had gone into industry and lived with a woman three years his senior and equally a high-flier.

The weather had turned colder and although the winter solstice was weeks ago, the days seemed shorter than ever. Rose was taking a mid-morning break, drinking coffee in the bay window as she often did. The sky was leaden and the light was strange. She was wondering if there was that rare possibility of snow when the telephone rang. She walked across the room to answer it. The last person she was expecting to hear from was Jack.

'I've been away for a few days. How was the party?'

'It went really well.' She felt strangely tongue-tied.

'Would I be interrupting anything if I came over?'

'Don't you have work to catch up on?'

'No. I'm not due back until tomorrow.'

Because she had nothing better to do, Rose agreed. Jack said he would be there in ten minutes.

There was an awkwardness between them when she let him in and neither of them seemed to know what to say.

'I've been to see the boys. They're both well.' Jack was fully aware of the tense atmosphere but was unsure why it existed.

'I'm glad. Do you want some coffee?'

'No, thanks. Rose, this isn't public knowledge until the lunchtime news but Alec Manders has finally confessed he killed Jenny.'

'Oh, Jack. How could he?' She was filled with sadness that Jenny's own father had taken her life. 'Had you guessed?'

'No. Not exactly guessed, but I did wonder whether it was possible.'

'Why?'

Rose hooked her hair behind her ears in a businesslike manner which Jack knew meant she was going to put him right on a few things. But he was wrong. 'Because I couldn't really believe it was anyone I knew.' She blushed with mortification. In fact she had decided Stella may have done it. 'Well, to be honest, I didn't want to believe it. Did you really believe it was Nick?'

'Yes.' Rose saw the spots of colour on Jack's cheekbones and knew that he had his reasons, personal ones, for wanting the opposite from herself. 'But I always had it in mind that it was possible that Alec had killed Renata all those years ago, that she hadn't really gone away,' Jack continued, hoping he was misinterpreting the smug expression on Rose's face. If she's worked it out, I'll kill her, he thought. 'I think I will have that coffee after all.' Something stronger would have been preferable but it was too early in the day. Rose got up to pour it.

'Thanks. We knew that Jenny confided in Maddy Duke and Maddy, the second time we questioned her, suggested that Alec might have been having a fling with a friend of Renata's. This led us to think that he might have killed Renata either to be with this woman or on the spur of the moment during an argument over her, then put it around that she had left with another man. Everyone knew the situation, they wouldn't have questioned his explanation. Anyway, as we know, nothing came of the affair between Manders and Josie Deveraux.'

Rose turned away to hide a knowing grin but she was too late, Jack had spotted it. The look of astonishment on his face told her that he knew that she knew the name. But all she had had to do was ask one simple question to discover it.

'Our theory is that with Renata dead and safely in the shaft Alec simply sent all the relevant paperwork to Josie, who posed as his wife for the purposes of the divorce. There's no need for a court appearance in cases of mutual consent, especially after six years. A solicitor in London, where Josie had taken herself, would naturally assume the woman in possession of a marriage certificate, or a copy, and whatever other documents of Renata's Alec thought fit to send her, was who she said she was.'

'All right, but why would Josie Deveraux oblige?' Rose wanted to know.

'His wife was dead, Manders was free to marry again. But he couldn't tell anyone she was dead, not if he'd killed her. With an apparently legal divorce taking place six years later it gives him a perfect alibi. How could Renata be dead when she's agreed to divorce him? And now you're going to say why, then, didn't he marry Josie, and why did she help him in the first place, especially after all that time?'

'Exactly.'

'He didn't marry Josie because he didn't want to and had never intended doing so, even though she believed he did, but we think he was still able to use her because somehow or other she was involved, she knew what he had done or had even helped him do it. And this, we believe, is the reason we can't find the woman posing as Renata Manders. Before his arrest for attacking you, Manders had already warned her it was time she disappeared.'

'That's more or less how I saw it. I spoke to my solicitor and he confirmed what you just said, about not having to appear in court and that a divorce could be obtained that way. I gathered that Josie could have taken on Renata's identity from the time she moved away and would have been known by that name for years. Maddy told me about her. And, like you, I thought Josie Deveraux had held out hopes of getting together with Alec all that time but when he finally let her down she couldn't do anything about it without getting them both in trouble. Like you, I thought she must've known or been involved with the killing of Renata.'

'Rose, just stop there. You keep saying, "Like you, I thought". Are you trying to teach me my job? Are you trying to say I'm wrong?'

'Yes, Jack.'

'Dear God. I rue the day I met you.'

'Well, just think about it. Alec's admitted to killing Jenny, but what's his motive?'

'We'll come back to that.'

'Okay. So he's going to prison. He's not stupid, and I'm sure it's been made quite clear that if he holds up his hand to both murders things would go better for him. Then why is he so adamant he didn't kill his wife? I'll tell you. Because it's true.'

Jack groaned. It was impossible that with all the back-up and expertise they had at their fingertips they were wrong and Rose Trevelyan was right. But he had to listen.

'I think it's far simpler than that. I think Renata Manders is still alive.'

'What? Explain, Rose.'

'As I said before, because of Alec's denial that he killed his wife.'

'But there's only his word for it.'

'Have you found this Josie Deveraux?'

'No.'

'But have you been looking for her under that name or the name Manders?'

'Rose, give me some credit.'

'Okay, sorry. But shall I tell you how I see it? Think of the family history, the power that Alec's mother wielded over them all. She turned her daughter-in-law into a drunk and more or less wrote off her granddaughter because she couldn't bear to see her son happy with anyone other than herself. Imagine how she would have felt if, Renata having run off with someone else, another woman appeared on the scene.'

She has a point, Jack conceded. And a very good one at that.

'Let's say that Renata did go as everyone believed. Now the coast is clear Josie decides to make her move. Maybe she went to the house and created a scene or perhaps Mrs Manders found her with Alec. We know his mother had a violent temper and wasn't afraid to lash out. What if *she* killed Josie? Alec would have gone out of his way to protect his mother, even now, even after her death. If I'm right, he isn't lying, even if he hid the body.'

'That makes sense,' Jack said quietly. Rose was right, perhaps they had been making complications where there were none. But how would they get a man like Manders to own up to what his mother may have done? 'But a woman?'

'She used to hit Jenny, Jack, she was a strong woman. Maybe she picked up something to use as a weapon or it could have been accidental. Maybe Josie fell and struck her head. Anyway, at least you know who killed Jenny.' Rose frowned. 'You still haven't said why?'

'He won't tell us, although we now know that Jenny wanted to move back in with him and Angela.'

'He'd hardly murder her for that. All he had to do was to say no.'

'Yes. Unless Jenny had something over him and threatened to use it if he didn't agree.'

'What? You mean you think she knew the truth about Josie?'

'Possibly. Or maybe she'd come to the conclusion that her mother wasn't alive.'

Rose shrugged and stood to refill their mugs. 'But she

wouldn't have had any proof and all Alec had to do was deny it. No, there has to be another reason. Hold on, didn't Jenny spend some time in London, after she came back from Paris?'

'She did. But what we don't know is if she visited her mother, or Josie, at the address Manders had been given.'

'I see what you mean.' Rose leant against the edge of the sink. 'That means I'm wrong. If Jenny went to that address and discovered it wasn't her mother but her mother's friend then she'd have no difficulty guessing what may have happened.'

'Quite. Anyway, Manders has had experience of fishing and mining and he also has a van. He'd have had no trouble in disposing of either of the bodies, with or without help.' Jack lit a cigarette and looked around for the ashtray. Reaching behind him he grabbed it from the worktop. 'What I don't understand is why he thought you were such a danger to him.'

Rose thought about it. 'He'd met me, he knew I knew Jenny and liked her and Jenny probably told him about where I'd been painting. Then he spots I have ulterior motives for visiting him and begins to think I know far more than I actually do. Of course, he'd also have heard that I'd reported those screams and that the police et cetera had been out there to investigate. I can't imagine how he must've felt when you went back a second time and found the body. Naturally, he'd have blamed it all on me.

'Anyway, surely DNA testing would prove whether or not the two dead women are related?'

'It's in hand, Rose,' Jack said sternly, wondering if he

ought to recommend her services to the Chief Constable. 'I must go, Rose, I've things to do at the flat before I start work again tomorrow. And I really am sorry about your party.' He stopped, his hand on the back door. 'Those screams. They're not connected to the murders even though they led us to the mine. One of your friends has it in for you. Please be careful, Rose.'

'I know who it was. Can we forget it? She's having treatment now.'

'I was right. It was Stella Jackson.'

Rose did not reply. Jack took her silence for agreement and nodded but he still made no move to leave. 'Did, uh, did Nick come to the party?'

'He did.'

'I see.'

'Jack, I already explained I'm not seeing him. It's definitely over. He lied to me on more than one occasion. Whatever your faults, and they're plentiful, believe me, you've never done that.'

And with that ambiguous praise Jack laughed and went on his way.

# CHAPTER TWELVE

It was May before Rose was satisfied that she now had enough good paintings to make it worthwhile contacting Geoff Carter, the man whom Stella had once advised her against going to see.

Geoff turned out to be down-to-earth and shrewd, a businessman who happened to be interested in art. He scrutinised her work, made a few notes and said he would be in touch. Rose left his gallery bitterly disappointed that he had said so little but at least she had tried. That was two days ago and she had not heard from him since. The year was not, as she had hoped, turning out to be any better than the previous one.

There had been no word from Nick since her party, but Rose was not sorry. If their paths crossed she would not avoid him but she saw now that he was a child and in need of constant attention. Daniel had rung once, puzzled by the fact that she no longer visited. Rose had found it hard to give a reason but there was no way in which she would allow someone like Stella to undermine her confidence again. She made excuses about being busy and left it to Daniel to ask his wife for the real reason – if he hadn't guessed it already.

Peter Dawson had finally taken her to dinner. He was intelligent and entertaining company but her instincts told her to leave it at that. Apart from what he had told her about himself she guessed that he would find her fascinating as long as she remained unobtainable but if she allowed herself to feel anything for him she would end up hurt.

She was at a loose end. Laura and Trevor had gone away on holiday and would not be back for another week. Jack was in Plymouth on a course and Barry was tied up on various plans for the season which had started with the Easter weekend but would not be in full swing for another month or so.

Walking back along the Promenade after a trip to the library, Rose stopped to watch the sea, standing at a safe distance away from where it was sweeping up over the railings. It was a high tide, the water choppy but topped by a clear azure sky. Further down children screamed as they tried to dodge the spray but failed. A pair of herring-gulls perched on the railings, their heads into the wind. They flew off, drifting in an air current until the dog which had run towards them scampered past, then they returned to the same piece of rail. I'm as free as they are, Rose thought, watching the gulls. And with that cheerful thought she walked on home to find a postcard from Laura on the mat along with a letter from her mother.

It was another four days before Geoff Carter telephoned, by which time Rose had given up hope of hearing from him again. 'How about the last week of June?' he said. 'If you agree I'll contact the local papers right away. There isn't much time.'

'Yes, that's fine.' Rose wanted to shout with joy. Had he said June the following year she would still have agreed.

'Have you got any more I haven't seen?'

'A couple. They're smaller.'

'Well, let me have a look at them. I can come to you if you like, it'll save you packing them up and driving in.'

'Thank you, that'll be great. Whenever you like.'

There was a pause while he checked his diary. 'Tomorrow, some time between four-thirty and five. Will that be convenient?'

'Yes. I'll see you then.' Rose hung up, unaware that Geoff had been about to say something else. 'Yes!' she cried punching the air. Tears of pure joy sparkled in her eyes. 'Hello?' She grabbed the phone which had started to ring again.

'Mrs Trevelyan,' Geoff Carter said, his voice deadpan, 'it would help if I had your address.'

Rose laughed and gave it to him, not caring if he thought she was scatty. It was one of the happiest moments of her life. I shall celebrate, she decided. But with whom? She could ring Peter but it might not mean much to him, having already established his own reputation many years previously. It had to be Barry, she realised. Barry who had supported her work all those years and had encouraged her to improve. He had always stood by her and he would be genuinely pleased for her.

He sounded harassed when he picked up the phone but

mellowed when he knew who was calling. 'You're treating me? In that case there can only be one answer. Best bib and tucker?'

'Nothing less will do.'

'Why?'

'I'll tell you later. I'll pick you up in a taxi at seven-thirty. Be ready.'

Too excited to think about work of any description, Rose rang her mother who could not stop telling her how proud she was. 'We'll come down, darling. We wouldn't miss it for the world.'

Rose said she would let her know the exact date as soon as she found it out herself. 'You have to be there on the opening night,' she insisted.

I can't stay indoors, Rose decided. Adrenalin surged through her. She threw on a jacket and almost ran down the path. She found herself nearly at the railway station before she realised how far she had come and stopped to draw breath. Checking her purse she saw that she had her credit card and rail card. Truro, with its shops, beckoned. A new outfit was required. She would wear it this evening then save it for her opening.

As if her luck had changed all at once, this mission was soon accomplished and Rose returned with three plastic bags. She had purchased a calf-length cream dress. It was sleeveless and hung simply from the shoulders. To go with it was a lace jacket in a darker shade of cream. The third bag contained strappy shoes with two-inch heels and a small matching evening bag and she had not even blinked at the prices.

Barry's eyes widened with surprise twice in quick succession. First at her outfit, which he said was stunning, especially with her auburn hair flowing over her shoulders, and secondly when she told him she was taking him to Harris's, a restaurant where media people ate when they were filming in the area. But when they arrived and Rose ordered champagne and told him her reasons he took both her hands in his and kissed her hard. 'I am so thrilled for you,' he said. 'I always knew you'd make it.'

'I haven't exactly made it, but it's a start.'

They were in the upstairs bar, picking at olives and crisps as they sipped their drinks. Having been shown down the curved stairs to their table they talked all evening in the way of old friends and Rose found herself feeling closer than ever to Barry.

'And now you must allow me to escort you home. I'll get the taxi to drop me back afterwards.'

Rose almost floated into the house. And tomorrow Geoff was coming to look at the rest of her work and finalise the details of her exhibition. She felt there was nothing more she could wish for.


'They're good,' he said simply and without exaggeration. 'We'll exhibit these as well. You'll need to get some invitations done for the preview. We can hold up to sixty guests.'

'I don't think I know sixty people.'

'Well, whatever. How do you want to play it? Wine and food or just coffee and biscuits? It depends on what you can afford.'

'Wine and food.' If it turned out to be her only exhibition at least she would have done the thing properly. 'Thanks for coming, Geoff.'

'My pleasure.' He hesitated, his hand on the kitchen door. Rose waited but he did not speak. Instead he glanced back over his shoulder and smiled.

It was after six but the evening felt more like summer than late spring. The change had occurred all of a sudden. One minute it was winter, the next there were days like this. Rose sat at the kitchen table and wrote down the names of everyone she could think of, even casual acquaintances. She would invite them all to her opening night. The shadow of a figure passing the window slid across the table. It was Jack Pearce. She beckoned for him to come in.

'Busy?' he asked, seeing her list.

'No.' She told him her news and said he would receive an invitation.

'I'm honoured. And well done, Rose. I really mean that.'

'You look better.'

'Better?'

'Mm. Less tired than last time I saw you.'

'You mean more handsome.'

'Honestly, Jack.'

Rose thought back to January and the day Jack rang to tell her that Renata Manders had been found. She had not received Alec's letter because he had not written. Renata had been in Scotland staying with friends for the whole of the Christmas period. Only upon her return did she learn of the death of the daughter she had never really known and the fact that her ex-husband had killed her.

She had travelled down to Cornwall to visit the grave.

'And did Jenny visit her?' Rose had asked.

'Yes. Once. But they didn't hit it off at all. That's the odd thing, Renata claims she didn't say anything particularly derogatory about Manders, only that he treated her badly and was having an affair, but Alec has now admitted that when Jenny asked to be taken in by him and he refused, she said, "I know what you did. How can you live with it?" She meant driving her mother away, but he thought there was a more sinister meaning.'

'Why wasn't Josie missed at the time?'

'Only child of parents past the prime of youth. Father dead, mother senile and in a home for the elderly in Devon. Once we had the DNA results we spoke to Manders again. We knew by then it wasn't Renata but it still could have been a stranger. This time he came up with the goods. His mother knew what Josie was up to and thought Alec might be keen to go along with it and move her in. There was a row, as we suspected, but Josie didn't fall, Agnes struck her with a poker.'

'My God. But wouldn't that have shown up on the postmortem or whatever it is you do with bones?'

'Not necessarily. It depends upon where the blow connected with the skull, and there were many other post-mortem injuries.'

And Renata had gone to London with a man who had befriended her whilst on holiday in Cornwall. They were still together, although Renata refused to marry him. 'Never again,' she had told the police.

Rose had said to Jack at the time that if Renata had taken Jenny with her she'd still be alive.

'Probably, but even that's not certain,' he'd replied. 'Fate is a strange creature.'

Rose thought back to her years with David and knew it was true. Jack had gone on to explain that Manders had made a mistake, he had wanted Jenny unconscious when he put her in the water to make it look as though she'd drowned, but had not realised his own strength. There had been no love lost between father and daughter and, Jack had said, more murders were committed amongst families than otherwise.

It's in the past now, Rose told herself. And now it's time to celebrate. 'Would you like a drink? To my success?'

Jack's expression showed that he was astonished she had not got one in front of her already. 'Good idea. Thanks.'

'Cheers,' Rose said, handing him a glass of chilled white. 'Here's to us. Things seem to be working out well for us both.' Jack had had some good results workwise.

'Not as well as I'd hoped in some directions,' Jack said morosely. 'How's Peter?' He was not sure how she would take this but he could not stop himself from asking.

The cuffs of the baggy shirt Rose was wearing had slipped down over her hands. She took several seconds in which to fold them back. 'I don't know. It's ages since I've seen him. To be honest, Jack, I don't have the inclination to keep in touch with any of them. Only Maddy. She's a different person now. She's heard from the adoption people, you know. It's only an initial inquiry but it's a start and it's given her so much to hope for. I'm praying the girl won't change her mind about contacting her mother.'

'Yes, let's hope not.' Jack studied his fingers. 'Rose,

would you let me take you out to celebrate? Just dinner. No strings attached.'

'Thank you, I'd like that.' She took in his handsome face, his large, well-formed body and his strong hands, recalling how they had felt on her own body, and was sad that, although for her it was over, Jack still wished it was otherwise. But they would probably end up killing each other if they lived under the same roof. 'Jack?'

'What is it?' He smiled kindly at the look of concern on her face.

'Thank you for being my friend.'

'I'll always be that, Rose. Always.'

She nodded. 'I know. And me yours.' There were a few beats of thoughtful silence before Rose looked up, excitement in her eyes. 'Anyway, did I tell you what Geoff said?'

Jack groaned and put his head in his hands. Without meeting Rose's eyes he asked, 'And who the hell is Geoff?'

Rose grinned. She wasn't quite ready to answer that yet, but she had had the impression that he had winked as well as smiled when he had paused at her kitchen door.